MADE
OF
STONE

Book One: Satori Stone Series

Desiree M. Palmer

DEDICATION

To all the light workers, healers, and star seeds.
To all of the teachers, learners, and seekers.
To all of the mystics, meditators, and knowers.
This book is for us.

CONTENTS

ACKNOWLEDGMENTS

Thank you, Grandma for reading this and believing - even when I didn't - I should keep going. Thank you for telling me it was better than anything else you read. I have full confidence you are absolutely not biased in the least and I am not your favorite.

Thank you to Albert and Quantum Stones for your support and your beautiful blessings.

Thank you to my early supporters who kept encouraging me. Especially my family.

Thank you for all the guides along the way who kept pointing me in the right direction. Your arrows were swift and on the mark.

1 In The Beginning

Some people are born knowing they are destined for greatness. For others, the truth of their greatness is flashed at them in Morse code from the corners of coffee shops or the spines of great novels. Truth, for these souls, must be broken down into tiny digestible bite-sized pieces; because the reality of it all at once would be too much. Still, when you have greatness inside you, wanting to get out, it will. Rest assured, it always will.

Satori Stone's greatness began the day she was born, March 21st 1975, at 12:56 a.m. the precise moment of the spring equinox that year. Although, like the other flashes of insight throughout her life, this event went unnoticed by almost everyone. Everyone, that is, other than her mother. Her mother chose the name Satori in part because it was the title of a student publication on campus for poems and short stories. However, we are getting ahead of ourselves. For now, let's stay on the surface as the truth of Satori Stone and her greatness reveals itself in little digestible bits. Because if anyone would have told her, in the beginning, the whole journey of her life, she may never have agreed to travel.

Satori grew up in a normal home. So normal and mundane in fact she never knew her father. She was raised by a single mother. It was becoming abnormal these days to grow up in a home which had both biological parents under the same roof. Norman Rockwell moments of sitting around happily playing board games or enjoying bike rides and picnics in the park. No. There would be no fatherly memories for Satori.

She also had painfully normal school stories as a child born in the seventies, growing up in the eighties and nineties. She wore fluorescent leg warmers and a single-sequined Michael Jackson white glove on her right hand. In her room were posters of TV show icons, stuffed animals and of course, she had a clear phone with bright florescent wires and nodes. It was one of those phones with a cord, and everyone shared a party line. It couldn't leave the house let alone her room. This was back in the day when you could waste an entire slumber party prank-calling people about their refrigerators. She spent her mornings on the weekend holding two fingers on the record and pause buttons of her stereo trying to get the perfect recording of her favorite songs while listening to the top forty count-downs. Praying the DJ didn't talk over her favorite song. Still, recording the perfect mix tape was an art and a science.

She wasn't picked on in school, but Satori wasn't particularly popular either. She lived a remarkably invisible existence all her life up until this point. She had the normal round of boyfriends, the jock, the bad boy, the strangely sensitive. None of who really impressed her much. She had the normal broken heart from a couple guys along the way. Moreover, as you might have come to expect by this point, one treated her like a pile of dog dung stuck to the bottom of his shoe and she gave all her power over to him. At least until she found herself pregnant. Then she knew she had to walk away.

It wasn't until she became the keeper of a tiny soul when she finally discovered her own power. She knew there was no way she was going to allow her daughter to be treated and learn how to be treated by a foul unkind man. You could say her daughter saved her life in one sense.

You could say that, and you would almost be right. However, we aren't to the lifesaving part yet. Her daughter did get her on track, but Satori was going to be the one doing the lifesaving, the world saving to be even more precise.

Growing up, Satori envisioned many careers for herself, never a superhero mind you, nothing so grand. In 5th grade, she wanted to be a top executive. To help her on this path, she started carrying a briefcase to school instead of a backpack. Even then, she wasn't teased. She was lucky in this way. Most people didn't pay her enough mind to care when she was being quirky. Most eleven-year-olds at the time were exchanging notes with boyfriends; Satori was using a tape calculator to do her math homework because she liked to hear the sound. Soon enough she lost interest in this along with several other career choices. To be fair, she lost interest in most things in life and moved on.

Until she found writing. Her mother was an English professor at Winona University in Winona Minnesota. One day she discovered she could create entirely new worlds with words and a pen. She loved going into those worlds and living there for a little while. She could live in any world as long as she liked and then leave again when the whim struck her. No commitment. A new adventure every day if she wanted. She finally decided to major in English. She did not want to be a teacher like her mother, however. Satori vowed to write things people were going to read, lots of people. She would spend her nights and her daydreams wishing for this. It is all she could think about as she studied. People looking at the pages she typed. As it turns out, she got exactly what she wished for. Unbeknownst to her at the time, she was learning a lesson. What lesson? Be very careful what you wish for because you may get it.

Satori wanted droves of people to read her novels, to love them and long for them. She wanted people to beg for more. But all she could see in her mind was people staring at the pages she had written. Which is exactly what she got. Many people did read the things she wrote.

After college, she did what any normal unnoticeable want-to-be writer would do while waiting for their novel to be born from them. She took a temporary full-time job just out of college in a place a few states away. She moved to Wichita Kansas to become a technical writer. If you have never heard of technical writing, you would be like most people in the world. As a technical writer, Satori wrote user manuals and product sheets for a manufacturer of camping equipment. She also wrote training manuals and guides for the employees of the company.

It was dreadfully boring. Kind of like sitting and watching dust collect on a treadmill of good intentions. Knowing you should list it on Craigslist and cut your losses, but you also keep telling yourself one day you will start. Still, hundreds, if not thousands, of people read what she wrote. At the very least, saw what she wrote as they used it for kindling to start campfires next to the tent they just purchased. It was not the career she envisioned, but it was going to have to do.

In fact, Satori's life was going just about as well as she had ever thought or hoped it could be. It was drama free if not a little boring. In other words, perfect. Anything more and for Satori this could only mean one thing. Demise. Bitter and complete. It seemed, for Satori anyway, just when everything was going well a big ol' Texas-sized wrench would get right in the middle of her almost perfect life. She never much cared for wrenches. Texas either for that matter.

It wasn't as if she had anything against either of them. She just found them unremarkable. She equated them with salt and pepper. So incredibly ordinary they were part of everything without even thinking about it. Salt and pepper were on just about every meal she ever ate as a child. Moreover, after almost every meal she would find herself in the restroom, clutching her stomach and wondering if the food was even worth eating at all. Everything but desert, which sat on her stomach just fine and so became her very favorite part of eating. Later in life, she found out she was allergic to black pepper.

Apparently, a person, Satori specifically, could actually be allergic to something as ordinary and every day as black pepper. Who has ever heard of such an absurd thing? Nevertheless, there it was. She found she was violently allergic to everything normal. Including black pepper, salt, wrenches, Texas, and as it happens, her life.

The next wrench in her life was about to smack her in the face and she couldn't even see it coming. Still, this time it was different. This time the wrench was bringing with it a restart. Why a restart and not a reset? The main difference in a reset and restart is the degree of the entire event. A reset is a 90-degree change while a restart was twice as far. This was a restart; the kind of transformation which changes a person's life forever. The kind from which you cannot return. The kind, which if it ever happens, can only happen once in a lifetime. Or so you get down on your knees and pray it will only happen once. The kind that leaves you wishing for a moment of normal. The normal which, until this point, bored Satori into a state of monotony.

This life-altering, wrench flinging, 180-degree turning restart of destiny was crashing toward Satori. She was oblivious to every little hint of it. All the flashes, all the coincidences, all the inevitabilities. All the while not knowing, not even glimpsing, it was crashing toward her like a runaway freight train. It was coming. Like it or not. Moreover, her life, if she was even going to have one in the end, (yes, it was that big) was never going to be the same.

2 Going Home

In the middle of her normal mundane life, things began a path into the bizarre, the magical, the mystical, and even the spiritual realm. It was Christmas break 2011 Satori and her daughter Sarah who was now eleven years old had gone back to Winona to spend the holiday with her mother Joyce.

Eleven is a curious age. Depending on when your birthday falls, you might be in 5th or 6th grade. The difference is quite dramatic at least it seemed so for Sarah. If you were in 6th grade, meaning you turned five before August of your kindergarten year, you would be enjoying your first year of glorious middle school. At least doing your best to enjoy it assuming you weren't covered in warts or have some other ailment for which children like to tease other children. As it happens, Sarah was in fact completely normal. She was not teased regularly, and not by people who weren't her friends, in which case Sarah didn't mind.

However, Sarah was not a lucky one in birth dates. Her birthday was in September. Being born in September meant you waited an entire year to start kindergarten and finally started when you were almost six years old. You were a full year older than all the other little babies in class, at least it felt this way when your neighbors were finally in middle school and you were still in elementary. Sarah assumed this odd circumstance would continue her entire academic career. She was never really able to relate to anyone. To make matters worse, the kids who were her age and not obnoxious little toddlers were only in her class because they didn't have the smarts to pass one of the grades in elementary school... Ele-men-tary. School.

While all the other kids her age were with people more befitting her maturity, Sarah was stuck in 5th grade. Impossibly infantile 5th grade. With toddlers. Sarah wanted very much to be in Middle school. It was for this reason, more than any other, she was so happy to go to Winona that year. Because in Winona, she was not a baby in Elementary school; she was an eleven-year-old, with all the maturity and middle-school-ness her age demanded.

Satori also looked forward to Winona this year, but more because it meant she didn't have to adult nearly as much as she normally did. Her mother would do most of the cleaning, the cooking, and the taking care of everything. Satori often wondered why it was she longed so much to be an adult all those years as a teenager. No one told her how difficult it really was. Well, to be fair, they did try. As a teenager, she knew far too much to listen when they did.

Satori had tried for years to get her mom to relocate to Wichita with her, but her mom always said, "I am going to stay with my roots." Satori did miss her mother, but more importantly, she hoped for a little help. She was a bit misguided in that sense. Satori finally reconciled the fact her mother wasn't going to budge and had given up on trying to talk her mom into anything different. Wichita was a big and scary city to someone from a town like Winona. All you had to do was look at the new pack of kids each year at WU to see how different the world was. Different and scary.

This trip to Winona had Satori wondering if she shouldn't take up the cause again. She noticed how weak, tired, and pale her mother appeared to be this trip. She was still a vivacious little spit of a woman. Still, Satori wondered to herself if she hadn't started donating to a vampire coven, her mother just wasn't herself. Joyce was still on her toes mentally, quick-witted and clever when the opportunity arose. Nevertheless, there was something more, elder, about Joyce this year.

Joyce had purchased airplane tickets for Satori and Sarah this holiday. She always hated the thought of the girls driving the 9 hours from Wichita to Winona. Satori and Sarah, on the other hand, cherished the time where it was just the two of them captive to each other's attention. Satori felt like the time they spent on those roads trips to see her mom was some of the best times they had ever had together. Joyce, however, being more practical and wise, just thought how uncomfortable and boring it must be. What if they got a flat tire, or a belt broke or something? They would be prey to all kinds of sinister types.

So, Joyce insisted this year she wanted to purchase plane tickets for them. Finally, Satori agreed. Satori and Sarah actually found flying to be not as bad as they had envisioned. There was a direct flight from Wichita to Minneapolis, which cut back on their travel time considerably. They were even able to spend time in the car together as they drove the two hours to Winona from the airport. Their return flights were going to be leaving at 2 p.m. out of the Minneapolis St Paul Airport. They planned to leave her mother's house around 10 a.m.

It was 8:16 a.m. on Christmas morning and the three women were enjoying the last bits of their family tradition. Just finishing their Christmas breakfast of Pillsbury cinnamon rolls, orange juice, and bacon, Satori and Joyce sat down for one final cup of coffee together before the girls had to get on the road.

Satori always loved Christmas morning. In fact, she had never celebrated one away from her mother and their little house on the east side of Center Street between Howard and Ninth. Center Street was literally the middle of town. This could be the entire reason Satori grew up believing she was the center of the universe. Or her mother's doting. The University was just one block over from 468 Center Street. The house was small, but always had enough room. Honestly, it seemed a little empty for Joyce by herself. Still, she kept it full of knickknacks and travel souvenirs. They covered the walls and any shelf or surface she could find. She loved having her treasures near her. She also loved talking about each one and telling their story.

There was an ugly little gnome Joyce got when she

visited Norway. He lay on his back laughing. Joyce said she got the gnome because it was what everyone did when they went to Norway even though she thought they were dreadfully ugly. To be fair, they were ugly. They weren't like the garden gnomes you see in here America. Joyful, pudgy and full of spunk. They were more like trolls. Dirty and a bit scary. Plump bellies and ragged clothes. The one Joyce picked out was the nicest one she could find. He lay on his back laughing. His little belly stuck up almost as high as his nose and his hair was deep brown shooting out in every direction.

Another of Joyce's favorites was a wooden painted plate she acquired while in Panama. She was given a ticket to take a boat through the canal by a stranger one night where she was staying. The man said he didn't need it and thought she might enjoy the ride. Joyce did enjoy it, immensely. At the halfway point, they disembarked the ship and went into port. At the port, there was a beautiful little tourist building full of little shops and food vendors. They had dancers in bright fiesta dresses and everyone was wearing Sugar Skull masks. In one of the shops, she found the plate and just had to have it. It was brightly painted like the ladies' dresses with toucans, parrots and other birds she couldn't identify. She loved the folksiness of it. She haggled them down to almost nothing. Joyce was always so proud to tell the story. Like she had gotten away with something. Truthfully, she likely overpaid.

Satori was in awe of her mother's life before she was born. It sounded like so much fun. Travels and adventures. Everything Satori wrote about in her stories, Joyce had lived. Joyce referred to the time as BS, Before Satori. After Satori, her life changed. All of

Joyce's money went to raising her daughter. They did not travel much but always had everything Satori needed or wanted. Satori was convinced she hung on to those treasures so fiercely because her mom missed the freedom she had. The truth is she clung to them fiercely because she had grown up always wanting things she could never have. Now she could have things she wanted, she wanted everything. And I do mean everything. Joyce rarely even threw away the toilet paper rolls if she wasn't forced to. However, once Sarah was born, Satori could finally understand having a daughter was not a sacrifice at all. Unless it was Saturday morning. Somehow a little voice at 5 a.m. on Saturday morning still felt like a sacrifice for the first few hours. Joyce was excited when Satori grew out of the wake-up-early phase.

It was right during their cup of coffee when Grandma Stone got a serious look on her face and said she needed to say something while she had the nerve. Joyce didn't want to tell her daughter this news on Christmas, but it truly couldn't wait a moment longer. She was surprised Satori hadn't noticed Joyce's packed bags when she came in town. Satori had noticed Joyce's packed bags earlier in the week. She had mistakenly assumed this was Joyce's new storage place for toilet paper rolls. Things were getting out of hand, she thought to herself at the time.

There wasn't any easy way to say it, so Joyce closed her eyes, held her breath...

3 Mother

"Satori, I have cancer."

"Cancer!?" Satori spluttered out. Getting coffee all over her mother's sofa. It was a good thing she always kept it covered in bath towels and plastic wrap.

"I thought you were going to tell me something like you are going on a trip to England. Maybe you decided to take up ballroom dancing even. Not cancer. Mom!" Satori was in disbelief.

Instantly, Satori knew why her mother looked so pale and obviously had lost weight. She thought it was her mother's age catching up to her. Now she knew that wasn't it at all. The hollow eyes, the pale skin, the thinning hair. Why hadn't she seen it sooner? Satori wondered.

Joyce told Satori she wanted to go on her own terms. And why not, Joyce had always done things this way. Joyce never much cared for rules unless they were her own. For her, a peaceful ending included enjoying the last bit of her life with her daughter and granddaughter. Joyce explained she wanted to live comfortably as long as she could and when she couldn't, she had already secured some medication she would take to end her suffering. She also let Satori know she booked three flights on the plane home and would be going with them back to Wichita.

Satori was finally getting her mother in Wichita but rather than allowing her to adult less, she was going to have to adult a lot more than usual. It wasn't the adulting which bothered her of course. It was the leaving. Her mom was leaving. Joyce wasn't sure how much longer, but the doctors guessed it would be a couple of months.

At 10 a.m., Satori loaded up the car and all three of them drove to the airport. They were just getting ready to leave when Joyce began to choke up. She asked to have a few minutes alone in the house. She looked at Satori and said, "You have been the greatest gift I ever received. I will never be able to say thank you enough." Joyce's eyes had become soft and blue. It was amazing, Satori and Sarah both noticed her eyes.

They allowed Grandma Stone some space to say goodbye to her home.

Since the house was paid off, Joyce was leaving it to Satori. Over the next few weeks, she would ensure Satori knew it was hers now and recommended she rent it out to college students to give herself a second source of income.

Joyce took her time visiting each room and thanking it for providing a place for her life to unfold. Starting in her bedroom, Joyce opened the nightstand

and took out a book. It was an incredibly special book. Joyce felt as though her entire world was in that book and everything that was ever of any importance happened on those pages. She would spend hours reading it. The same parts over and over. The beginning was her favorite, although it was difficult to pick a favorite with so much from which to choose. It is just beginnings; well, is where everything starts, isn't it?

She carried the book with her as she moved throughout the house giving each room its due. She saved the living room for last. Not because she loved it most, but because she was leaving her favorite book there for Satori to find after she was gone.

After she was gone. It was a thought, a sentence, a period of life she couldn't be part of. Joyce had spent exactly four months, twelve days and two point five hours preparing for. Right after she threw up in the doctor's trash can when he told her the news. It was just a damn lump, she had insisted. Nevertheless, the doctor wouldn't come off his proclamation. As it turns out it was one of several lumps. Several lumps had made their way throughout Joyce's body entirely without her permission or knowledge.

She walked over to the wagon wheel coffee table with her book clutched tightly in her hands. Moving her figurines to the side, she placed the tome reverently on the glass surface. Her eyes welled up. She so wished she had the courage to share this book with Satori while she was alive, but she simply didn't know how. Therefore, here it would sit until Satori came back. After Joyce would have nothing more to say.

Waiting in the car for quite some time, the girls

started to worry. Satori was just getting ready to check on her mother when the front door opened and Joyce came out holding her handbag and handkerchief.

Satori looked at Joyce understanding her mother was coming to grips with the fact she was dying and would never see her home again. How difficult that must be she imagined. Very adult. Then she wondered, "How the hell do you say goodbye to your mother?" Very, very adult she surmised. She realized then, more than before, she was getting ready to learn. "This is one big damn wrench, thanks for nothing life!" she thought to herself.

On the drive to the airport, Satori couldn't keep the tears away. Joyce held her hand as they had done so many times when Satori was younger. Joyce used her other hand to comfort by patting gently on the mound of flesh and bones gathered on the center console. Joyce softly spoke words she hoped would soothe her daughter's heart.

"Satori, don't be sad. Don't fill today with sadness. There will be a time to cry. A time to mourn, but it isn't now. Let tomorrow's worries wait until tomorrow arrives. All you have is now, and right now, I am here, beside you. Let us enjoy each other. Let's smile and laugh together as much as we can. Save those tears for when you need them." Things went this way for the next two months. Both women pretended to be strong while Joyce continued the path she had chosen.

Luckily, there was one adult in Satori's life she could lean very heavily on for this ordeal. Her next door neighbor, Naoma. Naoma was retired and independently wealthy. Not the kind of retired you are when you're old and too tired to enjoy it. Naoma had retired in her early forties. She had already enjoyed more than a decade of not having to work and enjoyed having a purpose other than her own musings. She was also not the kind of wealthy with private jets and seasons in different homes. Her wealth allowed her to enjoy her life if she lived modestly. It was enough; Naoma would say. Satori thought, "I would like to know how much enough is." Because she had never understood feeling how much money was enough, not ever, not even once.

Satori was however especially thankful for Naoma these days. While Satori worked, Naoma would check in on her mother and make sure she was doing okay. One day a few months after she had arrived in Wichita, Joyce was feeling especially weak. She couldn't make it out of bed, not even out of her pajamas. It was on this day Naoma knew it wouldn't be long before she took the pills she had brought with her from Minnesota. She sat down beside Joyce's bed in the middle bedroom of Satori's house. The one she had made especially for her mother with lots of shelves and cabinets for knickknacks.

Naoma knew the day had come for her to reveal the truth to Joyce. She took her hand and placed their folded hands on her heart. She asked Joyce to close her eyes and allow her to send comfort with her energy. Naoma closed her eyes as well and took a deep cleansing breath. Naoma then shared with Joyce all the truths she knew. She shared with her love and gratitude. Naoma shared with her, the comfort Joyce had needed to make the very last decision she would ever make in her life.

Joyce didn't understand what was happening at

first. Well at any point, actually. She settled into the moment with ease. She didn't understand how she could be seeing this movie in her mind, as if she was there herself, only she knew she wasn't. She didn't understand how these visions were being given to her when they weren't hers. She didn't understand why she was seeing any of it. Then she saw the one thing which tied everything together. It was all clear. With that clarity, Joyce began to weep.

When Joyce finally opened her eyes, it seemed like hours had passed. They were filled with tears and so much love was beaming from her heart. So much love Naoma could see Joyce glowing. Joyce knew it had to be near evening time by now. She did her best to look through the puddles in her eyes at the clock worried Satori or Sarah might be home soon, only to realize it had only been a couple minutes. It was as if time had stopped while Naoma sat with her.

Joyce looked at Naoma and told her "thank you," very gratefully. She squeezed her hand and said, "It's time. Tonight. I am leaving tonight. You have no idea what you have done for me." Naoma just nodded and said, "I will leave you for now. Thank you, Joyce, for allowing me to bless you in this way." As Naoma left the room, Joyce called to her. "Promise me you will be here for the girls now."

"Of course, I will Joyce. How could I not be?" she responded.

Then Joyce told her about the book she left for Satori to find. She told Naoma she was unsure if it was the right decision now. What if it was too much for Satori to handle? She asked if Naoma could help ease the way for Satori like Naoma had done for her. Naoma responded, "Joyce, we all have to follow our path. Satori will learn what she needs as she needs it." She assured her if Satori asked for help, she would provide it, but she must allow Satori to travel her own road. Somehow, Joyce understood completely.

That night, Joyce said her goodbyes to Satori and Sarah. She told them, she was finished with the suffering. They held each other tightly until finally Satori and Sarah could both agree to allow her to move on. Joyce took the medication she had been guarding and silently quietly feel asleep with Satori and Sarah by her bed. Joyce took her final breath at 12:16 a.m. on March 20, 2012. Just one day before Satori's thirty-seventh birthday.

4 Grief

While massive and important Joyce's passing was only the tip of the glacial wrench headed toward Satori. And while she was beginning to understand her life was in turmoil, she still had no clue of the enormity. Satori mistakenly thought everything was over.

What more could someone expect at this point? What more can God put on the shoulders of one single person, she thought. Losing your only parent, your rock, the last and only anchor to your past. Having your foundation ripped from under you, being forced to root yourself in the ground for a new foundation on which your future generations will grow and flourish. Learning to honor that which you were taught as you are still grieving and that which you lost when you still can't begin to comprehend the full magnitude of it all. No, nothing more can come to a person in this broken state. In fact, she would learn, there can.

Joyce wouldn't be the cause of any more burdens for her daughter; if she could help it. She had taken care of everything, so Satori didn't have to. Joyce couldn't find any good reason to rot in the ground, and she certainly didn't want her bones alone in Winona. Joyce wanted to be cremated and Satori honored her wishes by having a small memorial service at the house. It was mostly people Satori and Sarah knew rather than people Joyce knew but a few of Joyce's friends did come in.

Satori's best friends from when she first moved to Wichita, Nicole came in support. Nicole also brought her oldest daughter, Alexis. It wasn't the kind of thing you bring kids to, but Alexis offered a welcome distraction for Sarah. Alexis and Sarah were good friends; they had been since they were babies. Nicole left her other five children at home. Ranging in age from three to thirteen, Satori swore Nicole was a superwoman. Satori had a tough time taking care of her one daughter some days.

A few co-workers showed up from the university. At least Satori summarized those are who the strangers were. She couldn't believe they made the trip all the way from Minnesota for the funeral. She didn't recognize them, but all were welcome.

There was one guy in particular who caught Satori's attention. It seemed as if he was staring at her and every time Satori looked at him, he turned away. When everyone was making their way through the family procession, the stranger stopped in front of her and took her hand. He looked into her eyes, almost as if he was looking for something. Satori's skin prickled all along her arm and not the good kind. He creeped her out. The man did not say a word. Just walked on. This was odd as most people were hugging her and saying how sorry they were for her loss. Still, Satori didn't mind not having to hug him. He was like a stick she thought. So skinny and lanky. His skin dark and dried from what she could only imagine was a long life of working in the sun. She would think about this man later and realize she couldn't describe his face at all, just his hand on hers and the cuff of his arm. Even after he had stared so deeply into her eyes.

Later at the memorial, she saw him talking with Naoma in the front corner of the living room. Naoma's back was to Satori so she could not make out what was being said. Satori thought he looked annoyed. However, moments later the man picked up his coat and left without even a goodbye.

Satori didn't mind either. He was odd. And she had about all she could take of people saying how sorry they were. She figured it was one less. Satori knew they were trying to help but remembering her mother as an absence, made Satori miss her even more. She was so empty inside. She wondered how a person could be so full of a hollowness. It couldn't be described with any reverence for truth.

Satori went to a dark place after the memorial. She put her mother's ashes and a couple of Joyce's favorite treasures on a shelf by the fireplace. She cleaned out the room, boxing up everything of her mothers and putting it in the shed out back. She even bought a new comforter set and donated the old one to the thrift store. The only piece of Joyce left in the house was on the shelf beside the living room fireplace. Satori saw this shelf and its sorrow every time she came home. It isn't as if she didn't want to remember her mother, she did. It was remembering her and all she had now lost was more than she was ready to handle. She felt like she had to suffer the loss of her mother over and over again every time she came home from work.

She thought about moving the artifacts somewhere less seen. However, in the end, she left them where they were. Satori felt as though she was admitting defeat or lessening the place her mother held by moving them. So instead, she put off coming home as long as she could in hopes being too exhausted to mourn would help. She came up with any excuse to avoid coming home and the memory of what she had lost. The problem with her grieving logic was she was also forgetting what she still had. Sarah.

Sarah had lost her grandmother. And at the impressionable age of eleven had to face the reality she too would one day lay her own mother to rest. Sarah was broken just like Satori, but she didn't have the luxury of avoiding her home. In fact, what Sarah truly wanted and needed was her mother, who should have been at home. All summer she spent waiting on her mother. Waiting and wondering and starting to believe she is what Satori was avoiding. So, Sarah did what any self-respecting almost teenager would in the same situation. She started hanging out at the neighbors. Luckily, for Sarah, her neighbor was Naoma. She wasn't as young and spritely as Sarah's friends from school, but Naoma made good company. Sarah had always spent the afternoons with Naoma after school. She loved learning about all the things Naoma had around. They were all so interesting. She had crystals and old books. Sarah loved to touch everything, they felt alive. She made tea with real herbs and honey. Everything was a moment of teaching for Naoma. It was all stitched in time by a little woman who appreciated the company of a young protégé.

Even Naoma couldn't help but wonder and worry

about how absent Satori had been in the months following her mother's death. Naoma didn't mind taking care of Sarah, she really enjoyed her company. What she did mind was how it seemed to be influencing Sarah's disposition.

Satori wasn't worried about Sarah being home because she knew how close Naoma and Sarah were. She knew Sarah was safe and well cared for. If anything, that safety enabled Satori to drift further and further away from her responsibilities. Satori kept the shelves full of snacks and easy to prepare meals, but beyond this, she had all but stopped being a mother to her daughter.

Until one night when Satori came home late. It was long after the sun had set. The house was dark and Sarah was in bed asleep. Satori walked in from the garage doing everything she could to not see the relics of her mother. She turned on the dining room light and was startled into her skin. Naoma was there, sitting in her recliner with a blank expression on her face. Immediately her mind went to the worst-case scenario, something had happened to Sarah.

She gasped, "Sarah, where is she?"

It was a realization of sorts for Satori, in almost the same instant she feared she might have lost her daughter; she also realized she still had a daughter. The terror and frozen frenzy inside her mind was alive and concerned.

Naoma just looked up at Satori and said, "Sit down Satori, we need to talk."

Satori could tell it wasn't going to be a good talk, but she was also filled with a knowing Sarah was fine. So, she did as she was told, she calmed her nerves and sat down on the sofa across from Naoma.

She knew where this was going and sat like a scolded child. Head slumped already making excuses and remorseful promises reasoning, "I know I need to stop working so much. It's just so hard to be here."

Naoma asked, "How do you think it is for Sarah? She lost her grandmother and her mother on the same day."

Offended, Satori exclaimed, "She hasn't lost me, she could never lose me. I just have some big projects, it helps to feel accomplished, and like I can still do something useful. So, I have to work a Saturday now and then. It isn't the end of the world,"

Naoma looked at Satori through her soft purple eyes and said, "Being that girl's mother is something far more useful than you can ever imagine. You don't want to wake up twenty years later and realize you gave up the only job that mattered."

Satori quickly quipped back, "Are you saying I am not a good mother because I am putting food on the table and a roof over our head? No one else is going to do it!"

Slowly, Naoma responded, "I know you love Sarah with your whole heart. It's clear. To be honest, she is hard not to love. I am saying you are not behaving like a good mother when you spend so much time away from her. A child can't raise herself."

"She's almost twelve, Naoma, she is fine for a few hours by herself each day. Besides, she is usually at your place and not alone. Didn't you two do your Saturday shopping trip to the thrift store?" Satori tried justifying her day away from home. Even she knew it was a lousy excuse.

"Not almost, Satori. Don't you know what day it is?" Naoma trailed.

"Yes, it's the twent... Oh my god!" she exclaimed, "Today is Sarah's birthday. I forgot. I am the worst mother ever." Gasping as she covered her mouth in disbelief. How could she forget such a precious day?

"Well, not the -very- worst dear. Some mothers never show up at all." Naoma's eyes teared up with a deep knowing. "Nevertheless, your baby girl went to bed this evening with tears in her eyes feeling like she doesn't matter nearly as much as she thought she did to her mom." Naoma's voice trailed off as her mouth and throat tightened, she begged her eyes not to tear up for Sarah's broken heart.

Satori dropped her face into her hands and began to sob. More because she knew she was failing as a mother and partly because she was beginning to realize there was no way she was going to be able to make this up to Sarah.

Naoma went over and sat next to her on the sofa, bringing her a tissue and putting a comforting arm around Satori's shoulder. Naoma assured Satori she had done the best she could to make the day enjoyable for Sarah. She said she realized when Sarah came over this morning with a frown Satori had forgotten. So Naoma did what she thought was best. She made up a story. She explained Satori had called the night before and told her she had to work on Saturday and to please make the day great for Sarah.

Satori checked her cell phone and saw there were, in fact, several missed calls that morning from Sarah at the house. Satori in hopes of being undisturbed with calls of "I am bored" and "when are you coming home?" chose to silence her phone. It had worked too well.

Naoma explained how she took Sarah shopping at

thrift stores and she found several beanie babies she didn't yet have. Then they went out for sushi and Naoma treated her to a movie in the new 3D theater. They watched Finding Nemo at the Warren on 21st Street. Naoma said they had a long full day but she could tell Sarah missed having Satori there as any girl would.

While Satori knew Sarah's day had been full of fun and laughter with Naoma, she couldn't help but get a sinking feeling in the pit of her belly that told her what had happened on this day would be one of those pivotal moments in a young girls' life. One which would take hours of therapy to repair. Or an entire truck full of Ice Cream and Chocolate.

Satori spent most of the night figuring out what to do to repair her daughter's broken heart. She planned to let Sarah pick everything they did on Sunday, every meal, every event, everything. Satori also decided it was time Sarah got an iPhone. She didn't want Sarah to ever again feel she couldn't get a hold of her mother if she needed her. Satori remembered Nicole telling her she got Apple phones for her and Alexis because it has a locator app which allows you to ping the phone if they aren't responding. She uses it to get Alexis's attention, but Satori figured it would come in handy more for Sarah than for her. She was again reminded how grateful she was at what an awesome kid she was raising. At least would be raising again.

Satori knew she had a lot of making up to do. That night was a like a light bulb turning on for Satori. She got out of her slump and remembered what she had a lot to live for, the exact thing her own mother died for. Time together with her daughter. Satori determined she had grieved as long as she could. She was no longer going to let her broken heart keep her from being the mother Sarah deserved. The mother she had been before Christmas break 2011. Joyce had told Satori there would be a time for tears, Satori realized the time for tears was over now. It didn't mean she would stop missing her mother. It just meant, moving forward, memories of her mother would be ones of celebration and appreciation for everything she had brought to their life.

Satori also felt it was time to finally deal with what was waiting for her in Winona. The house. She needed to go back and pack everything up. She had decided to rent it out as her mom suggested. It would be like having a second income, well a small one anyway. And it was what her mom wanted. Since school was already in session, she decided the best time to go back would be, ironically, over Christmas break this year. The timing was lousy Satori thought. Then she remembered her promise to stay positive. She quickly stopped herself and tried to reprogram her thoughts. Rather than one Christmas, they would have two Christmas' this year. One in Winona and one in Wichita. They needed to start building their own traditions. Traditions which didn't include Joyce, or at least were built around her memory.

ousands place in the year calendars to roll over to a
00, the world, in fact, kept right on going. A
----- Sarah was born on the fall equinox and she was

Both times of year were perfectly in balance. Dark
and light, death and rebirth, yin and yang. Satori also
felt like Sarah coming into the world was a perfect
balance to her life. 2000 was in truth the best year of
Satori's entire life. The polar opposite of what 2012
had turned out to be. 2012 was proving to be the

worst year of Satori's life. So why then would she not believe everyone was right about the world ending.

Doomsdayers' all over the world, but especially in America, were hunkering down and settling in for the looming apocalypse. December 21st at 6:11 Central Standard Time 2012, the world was going to end. Or so the Mayans said. Only as it turns out, the Mayans never said so at all. The Mayans were getting a bad rap. The calendar they used was set to expire, and with the expiration of their calendar, so was life as the world knew it. Therefore, everyone who wasn't a Mayan interpreted this to mean the world would cease to exist. After all, we could never again know what day it was if the calendar of all calendars was going to end.

The Mayan calendar did end on December 21 at 6:11 am. However, it also began again, for another five thousand one hundred and twenty-six years. An important fact left out of many news reports until everyone was already half scared to death.

Because of this exceptionally large irritating fact, every person who heard when Satori and Sarah were returning to Winona would then make some kind of joke or foreshadowing omen. Depending on their perspective. Her boss, Nathan, was one who didn't get caught up in media hyped apocalypse stories would joke he was never going to see her again. This was unwelcome news indeed for Nathan. Satori's unbelievably bad year had in turn given Nathan a fast track to promotion because of how productive his department was. So not seeing Satori again meant quite a lot to him. More specifically, it meant a much less productive department. Nicole, Satori's best girlfriend, teased she booked it because Satori thought if they were in the air she and Sarah would be saved. Not one to be easily deterred Satori would laugh and say, "Well, if you don't wake up on the 22nd just know I told you so."

Truthfully, though Satori wasn't sure what to believe. Satori was a woman who had long ago made very good friends with paranoia. Such good friends in fact she had an on-again-off-again relationship with anti-anxiety medication. Currently, that relationship was off. She was stubborn and wouldn't let speculation, which was likely unfounded, deter her from getting back to Winona and taking care of things.

She did however feel December 21st coming with a force. The force controlling her destiny that day; however, was the 5 foot 4 inch tall Tasmanian devil slash organizer she had hired to ensure she stayed on track and got the house wrapped in the 5 days they had there. Nonetheless, not jumping to paranoid delusions of catastrophe was not her strong suit. Satori and paranoia were old friends.

When December 20th came, the girls packed their bags and headed to the airport. Even though Satori and Sarah loved their car rides Satori was taking a flight again this year. She was certain she would have loads of things to bring back from Winona after packing up her mother house. It was for this exact reason she decided again this year, they were flying. She was determined not to give way to her genetic pack-rat tendencies. Satori, while past the part which kept her in tears, was still very solidly engulfed in missing her mother. She knew she could easily move every single item from her mother's home to her own. The problem was Sarah and Satori were already making use of every inch of their own home. They didn't have the room to add furnishings from one three-bedroom ranch to their own already well appointed three-bedroom ranch. Flying would ensure unless Satori wanted to pay to ship the items home, she would only leave with what she must have. Satori thought it was a solid plan.

They went over to Naoma's to say goodbye and Satori thought she saw a tear in Naoma's eye.

"Oh, Naoma, you aren't buying into all this nonsense about the world ending, are you? You know we will be back next week." Satori probed as she reached up to wipe the tear from Naoma's eye. The two had become remarkably close this past year with her mother passing and missing Sarah's birthday. They had always been close, but guilt is the great equalizer and Satori was overflowing with guilt after the great birthday incident. After losing her mom, Satori just needed someone to lean on and Naoma was happy to step in.

"No dear. I know you and Sarah will be fine. I just wish I could be there to help you. December 21st is a big day you know. Maybe not in the sense everyone else is worried. I just feel like it is going to be a big day for you. Please, promise you will call if anything happens. I will be worried about you," Naoma remarked.

Naoma remembered what Joyce had told her about the book and leaving it behind for Sarah to find. She also knew what the book was going to reveal. She knew there would be a leveling in Satori's life. She knew how important it was for everyone to travel the path they were given, and she could not interrupt no matter how much she may want to.

"Stop being silly, Naoma, you are going to make me even more paranoid than I am. Which isn't difficult to do you know," Satori chuckled to her hoping to release her worry.

Naoma had always referred to herself as a mystic. Satori wasn't sure what that meant other than to know Naoma knew and understood a lot of things she had no business knowing or understanding. A lot of things Satori did not really understand. Naoma would always tell her, "You don't have to work so hard dear if you would just let me teach you a few things." Satori knew Naoma was well intentioned, but she was not always sure Naoma had all cylinders firing. Satori never dismissed her outright. She would just come up with something to do or place to be when Naoma would start saying these kinds of things. Naoma never pressed it and always had the same response. "We all must travel our own path, dear," with a coo of mystery.

The flights were for the most part, normal and ordinary. Which in these days of air travel translates into irritating. Everyone is packed as close as sardines; dry air which is somehow too hot and too cold at the same time. Satori was remembering why she really didn't like flying after all. There was one bit of unpleasantness, a toddler sitting behind Sarah's seat from Denver to Minneapolis. Satori had opted to save a few dollars by not taking the direct flight but rather having a layover in Denver.

Satori ended up trading seats with Sarah, because, well, Sarah is a moody preteen and after all, taking the hit, literally, is what moms do. As they traded, Satori gave the obviously frazzled mom a look of indignation trying to convey any self-respecting parent would keep their kid under control. It did not make a difference. And when she saw the mother's face, Satori knew she was beside herself with embarrassment and completely overwhelmed. Satori just kept telling herself, "This too shall pass." Nonetheless, each time she got a new case of whiplash Satori's resolve was tested. She was never as happy as the moment the pilot announced overhead, "Flight attendants prepare the cabin for landing."

Once they landed and picked up the rental car, they went straight to the hotel. She was exhausted after the day of travel and so was Sarah. Satori knew she didn't want to stay in the house. There were too many memories. So, when James and Dotty, the innkeepers at the bed and breakfast just around the corner from her mother, offered to allow her to stay at no charge she jumped at the offer. They had been good friends with Naoma often sharing a cup of coffee or tea in the evening when they didn't have guests.

To be fair everything in Winona was just around the corner from everything else in Winona. It is a small town on the west bank of the Mississippi just on the other side of Wisconsin. fourteen blocks across and about three times as long. Winona State, where Joyce taught for years, and St. Mary's University took up the entire town. Satori never did think there was nearly enough room for two colleges in the one tiny town. But it all somehow worked.

No one had been in Joyce's house since last Christmas. Rather than dealing with any waiting catastrophes like broken pipes or a mouse infestation, Satori wanted to get a fresh start in the morning. It had all waited a year and it could wait one more evening she surmised.

The girls pulled up to the Carriage House Bed and Breakfast around 7:30. The Edward's had saved the Friendship Room for the two girls, mostly because it had separate beds. Satori was very grateful. While she loved Sarah with every piece of her heart, Sarah could throw a mean sucker punch in the middle of the night. There would be enough trouble sleeping as it was with all the memories and work to be fought through.

The Friendship Room at the Carriage House had painted lapboards in an off-white color and old wallpaper covering the walls. The wallpaper was a cream and maroon scallop with dainty little baby's breath flowers in vertical alternating strips. The Edward's had remodeled the inn in the 80s when they decided to turn their home into a bed and breakfast as their retirement project. Satori was certain they were going for the 1880s in this room, but it felt more like a 1980s interpretation of the 1880s to her. Still, she was not going to complain. It was quaint and charming and just what she and Sarah needed. Sarah's only thought was how cool it was to have her own room, even if the room was the size of a closet and filled to the brim with her twin size sofa.

The girls settled in and went to bed early, ready to get a fresh start on the day.

6 Awakening

Satori was woken, too early to be kind. And far too early for a day of work that didn't start until 9 a.m. She wasn't sure what woke her, perhaps it was an earthquake although she doesn't remember any rumbles. She looked over at the clock and it was exactly 6:11 am. She thought for a moment. Wondering if she was woken to make sure and witness the end of the world. Maybe everyone on earth had been. But as her mind joined her in an awake state, she began to reason. She saw Sarah sound asleep with one arm and one leg hanging off the bed and heard her soft purring snore. Looking at the clock again, now 6:12 a.m. she came to terms with the realization the world didn't end after all. Everything was going to be okay. Life would be continuing. Then she had another realization. She was actually going to have to go clean out her mom's house.

Satori had made arrangements for a professional organizer to come help her stay on track. She assumed she would start getting sentimental and want to keep everything or worse yet, stop working and start crying. Maureen "The Cleaning Machine," as her website claimed was scheduled to arrive at 9:30. Satori decided there was no use in going back to sleep, she might as well get up and head over early. Sarah had planned to stay at the inn and help the

Edward's. They didn't ask for her help, but Satori insisted they let Sarah help with making beds and cleaning since they were allowing them to stay for free. Sarah didn't mind, really. She knew Dotty well enough to know after about two beds she would insist Sarah just find a quiet spot to study. And Sarah knew studying meant she would get to "read," but really play games, on her kindle. So, Satori got dressed and went downstairs for breakfast. It was winter, so she put on her favorite jeans, they were loose fitting medium washed denim. With a maroon long sleeve V-neck tee shirt. She paired it with a camel colored cable knit-cross front oversized button sweater buttoned at the left shoulder. She added a denim colored scarf with a fun tie wrap at the neck. She wore matching camel suede belt and boots. She thought the best plan was for layering and colors that wouldn't show dirt. After all, she may have to get dirty, it didn't mean she was going to have to appear uncivilized.

The Edward's were already up preparing breakfast by the time she made it downstairs. Since the girls skipped dinner the night before Satori was excited to see a delicious spinach and feta quiche, fresh fruit, and toast with homemade butter and jam waiting for her. Along with all the bacon, sausage, or ham she could eat. She had always loved Mrs. Edward's homemade jams; it was an indisputable bonus she was going to have some every day over the break. The entire breakfast was divine and exactly what she needed to start her day. She made sure Dotty and James knew Sarah was staying behind today to help. They just nodded their heads in passive agreement. They had a system developed over the years and each knew what to do to take care of everything. But it was going to be nice to have a youngster around to remind them what it was like to be so full of energy.

Satori felt a little queasy as she looked at the clock and realized it had only taken her ten minutes to eat breakfast. There was nothing left to do now but go to her mom's house. She couldn't help but think how bizarre it would be going home and her mom not being there. Going home and knowing her mom would never be there again. She really wasn't sure what her reaction was going to be, other than heartbreaking.

Satori pulled up to the house in her rented baby blue Hyundai Sonata. She was relieved to see at least from outside it did not appear anything was amiss.

Her heart was dragging on the ground as she walked up the tiny sidewalk past the untamed bushes to the front door.

I am going to have to trim those before I leave, Satori thought.

She put the key in the lock and inhaled her last untainted breath, deeply. She anguished at the three panes of glass on the front door, as she had so many nights she came home past curfew. Her silent prayer changed this time however, she used to pray her mother was asleep, so she could avoid getting in trouble. Now Satori still prayed her mother was asleep only now it was different. If only her mother was asleep inside, it would mean she was still here. Still alive. Still breathing inside these walls of her home. Not gone. And there weren't bits of her sitting on a shelf at Satori's home back in Wichita. Satori wished her mother could be asleep in her home even if it meant she would get scolded for coming home late.

Opening the door Satori could smell her mother in the air. At least every scent she had ever associated with her mother. She smelled Joyce as well as the musty odor of a home having been closed for a year. She hadn't realized until that moment her mom had a smell so distinct in her mind. It was comforting, almost seeming she as if was still there.

Everything was eerily in the exact same place; untouched by time, loss, or heartache. It was so clearly, exactly, the same. Usually, when Satori came home for a holiday her mom had some new treasure prominent in the front room, or she had painted a wall or finally thrown out and replaced an old chair. It wouldn't be the case this time. Nor ever again. She shook her head as if to get the thoughts and sadness to leave like a dog flicking off water after a bath.

"I am just going to think about all this stuff as someone else's. I will pretend it is not Mom's." Almost as if she was willing all the things in the room to obey.

Satori started to walk into the living room and suddenly stopped. She did notice something out of place. Not only was it out of place but she was sure her mother had put it there to tempt her to look in it knowing it was forbidden. On top of the wagon wheel coffee table was a book. Not just any book, Joyce's book. The one no one, especially not Satori, was allowed to look in or even touch. Her mind raced with thoughts, maybe this was just an elaborate scheme to test her. Like her mother really didn't pass, and she was waiting behind a door to come out and smack her hand. She looked around, wondering who was waiting to see her. Satori determined there was no way she was going to read it now; it was her mother's most adamant desire when she was alive for Satori not read it. She would not be tempted now just because her mom could not stop her.

Just then she saw a post-it note on top. She realized there a message written to her from her mom. The writing was almost faded, it had been written in highlighter and it was barely visible. Still there it was in written in plain English, daring her to follow her temptation, "For Satori, when I am gone. Mom"

She was frozen with wonder, gripped by fear, and trembling with bewilderment. She left this for me. To find. To read. But. I was grounded if I looked at it. Why? Why now? She pondered to herself.

Then she realized something even more disturbing. It had been waiting for her to find it for a year. Technically, 361 days. That means, anytime from when they pulled out of the driveway until this moment she could have found it. But why was it back at her mother's house, anyway. Why wasn't it with her, as it had always been with her? Why hadn't Satori noticed it was gone? If she wanted her to have it so badly why didn't she give it to her in Wichita? Now she finds it when the world was supposed to end. It was all too much.

So she did what any mostly sane partly confused daughter would do at a time like this, she scolded her mother. Aloud. For everyone within her house to hear. "And what if it had, Mom? What if the world ended today, and I never got this!" Because clearly, this was the most obvious item up for discussion. She found the courage from somewhere deep inside to finally walk over to the coffee table. Not to the book. That was not to be touched. Not yet. Satori had to settle in with the thought for a moment.

This was her mother's diary. Her mind had wondered many times as to what could be so scandalous Joyce protected it with vehemence. It was untouchable. A constant stream of "Don't go near it," "You'll be grounded" and "Damnit Satori what have I told you?" Joyce never cussed, so earning a Damnit was next to high treason. Even now she feared a slap on the hand if she were to touch it.

Bravely she reached out and put her fingertips on the spine. First just on the spirals. The slowly and carefully she moved over to the cover. Off-white with flowers crushed and dried in the fibers of the paper covering the hardboard on top. There was no swat. Not even a cold chill. Thinking it might be okay just to hold it she picked it up and held it by her heart.

Satori remembered how much she always loved looking at it. She even thought she could smell the flowers. Now she realized, it wasn't the flowers, she smelled her mom. Lilacs. Her mother smelled of lilacs. And so did her house. Why had she never realized this before? Maybe the absence of her made her scent try harder to be known.

Finally, with resolution, she sat the lofty book on her lap and slowly opened it.

There was a folded-up note, on which Joyce had written, "Read this first." Joyce spent three pages explaining to Satori much she loved her, how she had been a blessing, a gift, a treasure. She wrote to Satori why she chose not to tell about her diagnosis any sooner and why she hoped Satori could understand her decision. Joyce explained she always did the best she could and gave her daughter what she thought she needed. She also said she had been keeping a secret. It was now time Satori learn the truth.

Satori was terrified to read the journal now. Her mom's diary was always something private she knew that, but it was private with things like how she tried drugs in college or kissed a girl one night when she drank too much. It didn't have secrets. Her mother didn't have any secrets. So how could her diary? Was it even a diary? What was she going to tell me? My dad was someone I knew, we were descendants of the royal throne, and I might be called upon to take over at Buckingham Palace, perhaps I had a grandmother and grandfather, but she did not want me to know them? Then Satori realized making up stories was likely worse than what her mother was trying to say. There couldn't be anything so grand. This was Joyce Stone after all. Calm, cool, collected, and utterly, absolutely, completely, skeleton free closets. Satori knew this fact without a single doubt.

So, Satori began to read the journal.

TODAY I WAS GIVEN THE MOST PRECIOUS GIFT IMAGINABLE. I WAS GIVEN A BABY GIRL.

She heard this more than anything else growing up, her mother was such a sap. She assumed it was left over brain damage from her mother's hippie days of free love and smoking weed.

She continued reading.

I NAMED HER SATORI. I AM NOT SURE IF I HAD A CHOICE, SHE MIGHT ALREADY BE NAMED. A COPY OF THE SCHOOL'S STUDENT PUBLICATION, 'SATORI,' WAS LEFT ON TOP OF HER WITH A HEART SHAPED STONE. THE TITLE WAS CIRCLED SO I AM GUESSING HER MOTHER WANTED HER NAMED SATORI.

Satori froze.

Unable to think or do anything for a moment.

She was in a tailspin of denial and comprehension. "Her mother wanted her named Satori? With a heart shaped stone?" she said aloud. She just couldn't wrap her mind around what was being said. What was being admitted to? What were the implications? Satori continued reading in hopes it would somehow come together.

I WAS WALKING UP THE STAIRS AT SOMSEN HALL WHEN I HEARD A STRANGE NOISE COMING FROM A BASKET OF FRUIT SOMEONE HAD LEFT. WHEN I WALKED OVER I COULD SEE IT WASN'T FRUIT AFTER ALL, THERE WAS A BABY INSIDE, SWADDLED UP. THERE WAS A NOTE,

"Please take care of my baby.
Date of birth 3-21-75
Time of birth 12:57 a.m.
She cannot exist.
She will not exist if I keep her."

I KNEW MY PRAYERS FOR A CHILD HAD BEEN ANSWERED WHEN SHE CAME INTO MY LIFE.

I HAVE A FRIEND WHO WAS A MIDWIFE, GINGER, AND SHE CERTIFIED I HAD GIVEN BIRTH TO HER AT HOME. SHE IS THE ONLY OTHER PERSON WHO WILL EVER KNOW THE TRUTH. SHE WAS RAISED IN THE FOSTER CARE SYSTEM AND KNOWS WHAT WAS IN STORE FOR THIS BABY IF WE TURN HER IN. SHE ALSO KNEW HOW MUCH I WANTED A BABY OF MY OWN. WHEN I WAS YOUNG, I WAS TOLD I WOULD NEVER HAVE CHILDREN. I AM STARTING THIS DIARY SO WHEN I TELL THIS BABY ONE DAY HOW SHE CAME TO BE MINE, I WILL BE ABLE TO SHARE HER WHOLE STORY.

Satori finally realized, her mom was telling her she

wasn't her mom. There was some other person in the world who gave birth to her and then left her out, in the middle of winter; well, at the end of winter. Nonetheless, Satori surmised she had been tossed out like the trash on the steps. Her birth mother didn't even want her to exist or care who took care of her. Why didn't she find an adoption agency? Did that person even care who found her? She knew the answer. No.

The Mayans were right. A world did end on this day. Satori's world. A gigantic wrench had sailed swiftly and easily right into Satori's life. It started with her mother passing; now she was learning it wasn't even her mother who had passed away. It was someone who walked by a fruit basket and heard a noise. An entirely new life had just begun for Satori, one she would now have to learn to navigate. Without her mother; without any mother whatsoever. She could not even believe what was happening.

Satori continued to read the book and skimmed through the passages. Her mother had written about how much she had loved Satori. Joyce detailed every time Satori had done anything, had said her first words, took her first steps, won ribbons. She wrote about little milestones, and big.

She found several entries from Joyce where the burden of carrying this secret was more difficult than she had imagined. Part of Joyce didn't want Satori to know, out of fear of what might happen with their relationship. And part of her knew Satori deserved the truth. Joyce would excuse it away saying Satori was too young to understand. Later she would reason Satori was too old to find out without damaging her delicate psyche. Joyce made an entry at least once a year on Satori's birthday, March 21. Joyce would recap the year, the accomplishments, and talk about how proud she was of her daughter. Then in early 2011, Joyce wrote about finding out she had cancer. She wrote about the plan, this plan, to tell Satori about her real birth. She planned to spend her last months with her girls and prayed they would forgive her.

Satori was torn. She was heartbroken and grateful at the exact same time and in the exact same way. She started replaying all the moments of her growing up in her mind. "Wasn't there ever a chance for her to tell me?" she wondered aloud.

Ding Dong.

The doorbell seemed somehow foreign and normal all at the sometime.

Satori startled back into her presence, shook her head and looked at the door. It was Maureen, the organizer Satori hired. She was even more thankful for this decision than she had been the moment before. There was no way she could get through these next few days without help. Although what she didn't need was to feed on the drama of her life by explaining everything to this stranger, well intentioned as she might be.

Worried her mother's diary might be found Satori excused herself to the car and put the journal in the rental's glove box.

She made her way back inside and they got started. They were scheduled to work until five in the evening. Satori felt she was already finished with her day. So much had happened by 9:30 am on December 21, 2012. They worked nonstop making their way from one room to the next developing a plan and talking through how to tackle the task.

The crew found a natural stopping point that evening around 4:30. So when Maureen suggested they finish for now, Satori was immediately on board. Having Maureen there as a distraction worked especially well, maybe a little too well, they had not even stopped for lunch. All Satori could think about was the growl in her belly and the equally loud question in her mind.

No matter how distracted she was, she kept thinking about what her mother's journal revealed.

She had no idea where to start. What did she do with this information? Who can she ask questions? Who are her parents? Is there even a way to find the answers at this point? But mostly she worried what this revelation would mean to her life. Was the whole thing a lie? Who is she really? She certainly isn't the person she thought she was.

Even all of this, losing her mother and then finding out she wasn't born to her mother, was still not the whole wrench coming toward her. The re-start was barely at a crawl. Satori was getting a clue, life was in a tailspin. But she still had no idea how big this thing was coming for her. I mean, who would? Most people would think after losing their mother and then finding out they were left for the lost and found bin at school, they had been given their limit. The "you never get more than you can handle" limit was met. This person should be given a pass at this point, they should catch a break. Right? It's like life or destiny or common decency owed them some courtesy of letting up. Still, there would be no letting up for Satori. None of it. Satori was destined for greatness. When you have to prepare for great things, you must have huge battles. So the wrenching, it was still coming.

For now, clueless Satori agreed with Maureen to meet the next morning and continue. They met for three days. In those three days, they got everything boxed, bagged, sorted, and cleaned. Satori arranged for the Salvation Army to come by on Christmas Eve and pick up everything she wasn't going to keep. She and Sarah went over to the house early Christmas morning and Satori made their traditional Christmas breakfast, for the last time in her mother's kitchen. She and Sarah spent Christmas day and the following day repainting and neutralizing the décor. Satori finalized the paperwork with a property manager and the girls were finally ready to go back home.

The last things Satori did was to take some of her mother's things back to Winona University, she hoped they could be used by the professor who took her place, but really it was an excuse to stop by Somsen hall. She had seen it hundreds of times in her life. Traveled those stairs so many times with her mother as a child, as a teenager, a university student herself. And now as she stood on the top landing of a long staircase, she tried to picture where someone would have left a basket with a baby inside. There isn't anywhere with an overhang from falling snow if it was snowing that day, she thought. There are nearly twenty steps to the top, there is a chance no one would have found the basket being so high unless they had climbed the stairs. Moreover, what if the basket was in one of the two side areas? Satori stood there, wondering, where her life began. How was she found? She was wishing she could ask questions of the one person who had the answers. She sat on the stairs and cried. Even though she promised herself she had finished crying.

She found a new reason to cry. She was crying for the life she never knew, the mother who didn't love her and the little bit of life she had 40 weeks before she was left on those stairs. She cried for the baby, cold, shivering in the winter, alone, for how long. And cried thankful for the women who found her and gave her a home. Then she dried her face stood up and promised herself that would be all the tears she would give to the baby left on those stairs and her first mother. She had a lot left to do and a child of her own to take care of.

As the trip was nearing its end, Satori began to feel a little off. She was prone to paranoid delusions. But the hair on the back of her neck would stand on end, typically when she was at her mother's house. She wondered if it was her mother's ghost, but then remembered she didn't believe in that kind of thing. She also had noted several times a dark blue Chevy Impala would be parked on the street or following behind her. It was everywhere. Oddly. In front of the house, she even though she saw it driving in front of the Carriage House at night.

Her rational mind kicked in and she remembered where she was. In Winona, population 27,546, well 27,545 now. Of course, she saw the same car a lot. Winona is an exceedingly small town. The college, her mother's house, and the inn were all smack dab in the middle. It would be more unusual for her not to see the same car several times. Still, she kept Sarah a little closer when they were walking.

On Thursday the girls packed up to head home. Satori tried her best to give the Edward's a token of her appreciation. They would have none of it and insisted they stay again when they next made it to town. Satori promised they would and Sarah gave them both a hug goodbye. Satori stopped by the post office on their way out of town. As it turned out, she found five boxes of things she had to keep; and she was willing to pay to ship home. She even found the old copy of "The Satori" with its name circled and edges worn and ragged. She shipped all five boxes of her mother's treasures, and now hers, back to Wichita. Satori was heartbroken. Five boxes were all that accounted for her mother's life. Five boxes and one full grown child who wasn't really her child at all. Just borrowed, likely from some college kid who was too afraid to tell her parents she was pregnant. Satori wanted to stop obsessing over how dumped and rejected she felt after all she had a mother who wanted her. A mother who adored her. But, it was all too soon.

Satori also found it interesting just as Joyce did for so many years, she too was now trying to find the best way to tell her own daughter. She understood why it was so difficult. She decided when they got home she would go over to Naoma's and tell Sarah and Naoma together. Satori knew even if she weren't in the right state of mind Naoma could ensure the right message was delivered to Sarah. Naoma always knew how to say things. She just had a way with words.

7 Stranger Encounters

The flight out of Minneapolis didn't leave until after 10 p.m. They were taking the same route home as they did when they arrived the previous Wednesday. Minneapolis to Denver then Denver to Wichita. The direct non-stop flights were an extra $200 each. Satori wasn't going to splurge. This was a decision Satori was beginning to regret. Not only was she bone tired after the week of cleaning and sorting and painting and crying; she was leaving with a heavier life than she arrived. A life which had questions oozing out of the cracks made by a damn giant wrench being twisted far too tight. The weight of telling her daughter and of not knowing who she was anymore was about all Satori could handle at this moment. Another kicking crying toddler would likely send her over the edge. She was thinking the $400 increase would have easily been worth it at this point.

Sarah, on the other hand, was a typical tired and grumpy pre-teen with her earphones on. She was anxious to get home and finally open her Christmas presents. Satori brought her big gift with them and allowed her to open it on the first day. It was a new iPad Mini from Santa. Sarah didn't believe in Santa any more than Satori believed Sarah believed in Santa. Still, it was a tradition in their family, Santa always brought the big gift.

Sarah had a few unnatural fears. One of those was about germs unless they were her own. The other was a phobia about strangers. She was a bright happy and outgoing girl but only if you knew her. If Sarah didn't know you, you couldn't get her to talk to you. Stranger Danger was not a terrible thing for a 5-year-old. However, the fear did not seem to be changing. This meant Satori was always stuck in the middle seat on flights. Sarah would get the window or the aisle.

On their way home from Winona, Sarah was at the window and Satori was in the middle. It was a full flight. The sardine can was fully booked all the way to Denver. Satori thought she might luck out. When checking in Satori saw the seat next to her was the only vacant seat on the flight. She hoped to use the room and stretch out a bit. Still, Satori did not get her hopes up to high because she knew how her life played out. When there was room for a wrench, one would come flying. It was only a matter of time before the empty seat was filled with a vile sardine.

It was just when the flight attendants were readying to close the doors; Satori thought her luck had changed. The seat was still open. Satori looked behind her and there were no toddlers in sight. Maybe her luck was changing. No toddler's empty seat. This was going to be a good flight, for once, things were turning around for Satori.

She was so preoccupied with stretching out to the extra seat Satori almost missed the stewardess welcome someone on board. Almost. Quickly scanning the plane, she noted three empty seats. She mentally crossed her fingers watching with anticipation. The man boarding stopped to ask the flight attendant a question and then turned to walk down the aisle and find his seat. That is when Satori noticed the stewardess point right toward her. DAMN!

Taking in a deep breath and opening her eyes wide, Satori could not believe someone was stealing her windfall. There are two perfect other seats, two other people who didn't show yet. But for Satori, two other wrenches a.k.a. two other lottery winners apparently. Letting the realization seep in she closed her eyes and dropped her head in defeat. Then realizing she was in fact, in public, and the man probably just saw the reaction all over her face, Satori took a deep breath, put on the best please-don't-look-fake-smile she could muster and looked back up. Sure enough, heading directly toward her was the seat stealing, freedom crushing, get-your-own-damn-seat, goose pimple inducing man. Wait what?

As it turned out anger and defeat were not the most overwhelming feelings Satori had right now. She wanted to be angry and curse the gods, but the warm tingling sensation inside her was not allowing it. He was without question the most gorgeous man she had ever seen. He was a strong rugged salt of the earth kind of handsome. His face had seen a few years, but it gave him character. He was not a young

Abercrombie model, but she thought he could have been a few years ago. Without realizing, Satori's smile turned in to more of a gaping chin on the floor drooling mess. He was tall, at least six feet she surmised. Muscular but not in a busting-his-shirt-open way, just enough to know toned flexed muscles were there just under the surface. He had sun kissed skin and his dark hair was naturally highlighted. Satori found herself mesmerized and staring right into his striking amber eyes. How cliché she thought. Of course, he has beautiful eyes. She wondered if she was looking at some kind of demi-god. And his smile. It was half-cocked to the right side. It seemed half-wicked and half-saint. This stranger's smile was literally melting her. At least that is what she thought was happening when the sweat started to bead up on her skin. She realized the warmth she felt wasn't just on the inside; it was showing in the red tinge of her skin as well. She was now adding embarrassment to her list of transmuting feelings over the last thirty seconds. Satori urged to herself, "Pull yourself together, Satori." Oddly, she was no longer hesitant to share her seat.

When he got to her row, Satori smiled gingerly up to him. He put his bag in the upper stow away revealing the smallest bit of his stomach and the slightest bit of trailing hair from his navel. She gasped. Yep, he really is in good shape she thought. His stomach was taught and flat and his navel, well she never thought she loved a navel before that moment.

"Looks like I'll be bunking here for the night," the stranger said.

"Bunking here," Satori thought, "was he military?" it would certainly explain the physique and skin tone.

Wait, bunking here, is almost like saying he wanted to sleep with her. Instantly she flushed red again. She just knew he had seen her reaction and was mortified.

"I only brought the one pillow. Guess we'll have to share," she played, trying to unravel the tension. Satori was not an expert flirter. She was not even a novice flirter. Satori did not flirt. Not even a little. She wondered what the hell she was doing.

He laughed and sat down. The man got himself comfortable and put on his seat belt. The flight attendants were on the speakers now giving preflight directions. Satori tried to act interested, but how many times does one person need to learn how to put on a seatbelt? Satori glanced over to Sarah. Sometime between boarding and the handsome stranger arriving, Sarah had fallen asleep. So, Satori adjusted her daughter's blanket and tucked her in for the flight.

Satori always hated the awkward, "We are touching each other but are going to act like strangers" thing that happens on cramped flights, so she decided to introduce herself. Who are we kidding? It was the least of the reasons she wanted to introduce herself. Still, self-delusion is deliciously addictive.

"Hi, I'm Satori. Are you on your way out or on your way home?" Satori said as she reached out her hand to shake his.

He reached back and shook her hand. Instantly the hairs on her arm stood at attention and a flash of light or electricity shot between their fingers. She shook her head; there is no way that actually happened, she thought.

"Whoa, did you feel that?" His brow raised on one side as his eyes widened.

"Yeah, you too!" Satori mimicked his expression of shock. She knew it, this perfect man was sent to her and they were magically connected.

"I guess I built up some static electricity running to make the flight. Sorry about that," the man said.

Ohhhh. Of course, there is a logical non-psycho reason for it. Satori was really making a fool of herself. She internally started scolding herself.

Outwardly they laughed, Satori with a full belly and the stranger more politely. Satori didn't typically make a fool of herself over a guy, but this one had her all knitted up inside.

"Home," he said.

Dumbfounded, Satori replied, "Whaa . . ?" shaking her head trying to understand why he was just saying "Home" for no good reason. Then she remembered she had tried breaking the ice before he shocked her back to life.

"Oh, you are on your way home? Yeah, we are too. It has been a long week. I mean when isn't Christmas a long week, am I right? But, this one was really long, I mean, really long. I'm sure you don't care why. Sorry, I don't mean to ramble. Or to imply you are uncaring. I am just going to be quiet now." Satori crazy smiled as she took a deep breath after having just verbally vomited an entire paragraph on him in the length of 4 seconds.

She was wondering to herself what she had just said. He hadn't asked her anything and she was making herself look like a fool. She quickly turned her head before he could see her scowl at herself.

Then she started thinking how much better looking he was up close. And his smell. She wanted to borrow his jacket and forget to give it back. He smelled like, well being honest, and why not, he smelled like men's cologne. Delicious, engulfing, mind tingling aroma turned on every fantasy a woman ever had about strangers and airplanes. She could see under his t-shirt the slight indentations confirmed hiding under there was a rock-solid set of abs.

Her mind was lost in the middle of imagining his abs exactly when Satori realized, she was staring directly at his stomach. She also realized what it must look like to someone sitting directly beside you on an airplane when you are staring at their stomach. She looked up quickly, and he was looking at Satori with the now familiar half-cocked smile. He gave Satori a wicked little chuckle.

Trying to help him forget she was just wantonly looking at his private area she spluttered out, "So, were you on business or pleasure?" And immediately regretted asking a question that included the word "pleasure" after having just been caught staring at what appeared to be at his johnson. She bit her lip in fear she might speak again. Satori simply could not win. This is the moment she asked a stranger, business or pleasure. She thought to herself, "Damned Wrenches."

She was determined not to lose her composure again.

He responded, "I can't imagine coming here for pleasure, Minnesota isn't the kind of place that makes my bucket list if you know what I mean."

Then remembering Satori was there with her daughter it was his turn to be embarrassed about what he had said. "Oh, I'm sorry. I assume if you brought your daughter, you were here for pleasure..." he stumbled out.

Satori, having regained control of herself tried to explain. "Well, I wouldn't call it pleasure, but it wasn't business either."

The two strangers spent the rest of the flight talking about Satori's life. Her mother, the revelation in her mother's diary, Satori's worry over what to do, her wondering how to solve who her parents really are, and on and on. The man was such a great listener. He never even looked bored with her rambling. In fact, Satori noticed him smiling at her occasionally. Almost like, he was amused, but mostly he stared straight into her eyes. It was intimidating to Satori but liberating at the same time. She felt like she had known him forever somehow.

The pilot came on the overhead and announced to the crew to prepare for landing. Time had flown by. Satori was embarrassed to realize she just spent the entire flight talking about herself. It was liberating in a way, to get everything out in the open. She had been bottling so much up she hadn't taken the time to just release. She thanked him genuinely for listening. But now, she felt defeated. There was a gorgeous man who happened to land right in her lap and she decided the best thing to do was to talk endlessly about everything in her life that was going wrong. Suddenly realizing this man had turned out to be a wrench after all, she just turned her head to Sarah and started waking her up. Thinking all the while, "If I ever get things going in the right direction I royally mess it up. It is just who I am."

Satori's obsession had turned from her new found lineage puzzle to one of self-pity and defeat. She didn't understand how such an amazing guy could have been interested in a woman like her anyway. She was so painfully normal. She thought a guy like that could have any woman he wanted. Certainly, Satori. Nonetheless, he didn't, now, for certain. She'd made sure of it.

Satori was very normal in many ways. She was not thin, but she was not heavy either. She wore a size 8/10 and on a five foot seven inch frame it was a flattering enough size. Her hair was mid length and straight. When she was younger, she had bright blonde curly locks, but as she aged her hair had turned straight and mousy. It would frizz up in too much humidity and was a regular pain in the neck. There was nothing unique or interesting about her looks in any way. Well, other than her eyes. She often got remarks on them. Her eyes were tri-colored. They started blue on the outer rim, and then turned green in the middle and finally yellow on the inner rim. They were on the pale side so they stood out remarkably well from most other peoples. They did make for a striking gaze. Nevertheless, whoever heard of someone dating a girl because she had pretty eyes, or an adonis dating a girl for that reason anyway? Satori had some work to do on her self-esteem. However, this work would not be happening on this flight.

The flight landed, and Satori reached out to shake his hand and again thank him for listening to her ramble. Having already stood up to grab his bag, he reached down and shook her hand. ZAP! The electricity was back. They both looked at each other dumbfounded for a moment.

Then he grabbed his bag from the overhead bin and practically ran off the airplane.

"Great Job, Satori," she scolded aloud. She did not even know his name. She told him her life story and did not even bother to find out his name. No wonder he ran, she thought.

After waking Sarah and helping her sleepily wobble from the plane, the girls found their way to the end of the D gates. Flights to Wichita were always on the small planes, which meant a long walk to the end of the concourse when leaving from Denver. Satori and Sarah stopped to get a bite to eat from the vending machines as they made their way down. They arrived at the very last minute. It had been a tight layover, so they probably should have skipped the candy bars at the vending machines, but she never was very good at saying no to Sarah.

The girls approached the counter and the woman at the desk advised them their seats were going to be split up. Since they thought they were not coming, they had given the window seat away. The plane had a single row of seats on one side and a double row of seats on the other. Originally, they were in the double seats together. "Julie" as her badge proclaimed, reassured them they were still going to be beside each other but there would be the small aisle in between. Satori wasn't worried since they would still be together. It was a short flight and she just wanted to get home. Of course, Sarah wanted the single seat. So Satori took the aisle seat and the pair left to board the plane.

The biggest downside of this flight was you had to board outside. Particularly cruel in the middle of winter, at night, in the Mile-High city of Denver.

Their seats were toward the back this time. Satori was fumbling down the aisle double checking rows and numbers. When she located the row, she looked to give an understanding smile to the person she was going to annoy this time.

There HE was. She stopped in her tracks. Turned and looked around as if seeing the other passengers would somehow let her know if she was on the correct flight. She was trying to process what was going on. She again looked at the row, the seat, the God. Yep, he was there, just sitting and smiling. His half-cocked smile, though. Ridiculous.

He stood to help stow their bags. Satori got a reminder of his smell, which had somehow managed to slip her mind. He really did smell delicious. She wanted to devour him right there. Satori thanked him again and politely sat down. Sarah put in her headphones, oblivious to what was happening around her, and stared out the window lest someone might decide to talk to her.

Satori was determined not to say a word this time. She had made a fool of herself enough. She didn't even know they were going to the same place. She was embarrassed at how selfish she had been.

Refastening his belt, he turned to her and extended his hand. "Hi, I'm Darvey, Darvey Lavender. Are you on your way out or on your way home?"

They laughed. Both with their bellies this time. But now at least she knew his name.

8 New Beginnings

The girls arrived home a little after 4 a.m. Satori was exhausted but also felt more alive than she had in a long time. It's as if those electric handshakes filled her with energy. As it turns out, Darvey dug her. He enjoyed how she did not feel intimidated by him or felt she needed to impress him. Satori still was not sure if it was a good thing or a confirmation she made a fool of herself. Darvey liked it so much, in fact, this time when they announced the airplane would be landing, he asked for Satori's phone number and if she would like to have dinner with him Saturday night.

While Satori eventually overcame her, "Why do you want to date this mouse" doubt, she could not help but wonder if he was just being polite. Then she would remind herself of the electricity and his undeniable hotness. In the end, she just thought, "Screw it. I am going for it. What is the worst that can happen?"

Then on top of meeting a handsome guy who seemed to have his life together, another first for Satori, the girls drove home in an empty city. Satori loved driving in the wee hours in Wichita. Barely a car on the road, the city always felt so peaceful at that time of day. It might be the solitude of it all buzzing with potential. Whatever it was, it all energized her somehow. Even with the buzz from her adventure home, Satori was asleep about seventy-nine seconds after her head hit the pillow.

The next day Satori woke Sarah sneaking into her bed. Sarah was trying to sneak in at least, something she would always do on the weekends. Satori really wanted to sleep in if she could, but Sarah loved getting up early. Not too early Satori thought thankfully. But, early enough to be the reason Satori woke.

Sarah would have slept every night with her mom if Satori would allow it. However, Satori enjoyed not having bruises far too much for Sarah to sleep with her. Nonetheless, they both really loved these mornings. The girls would lie in bed for hours talking, tickling, and laughing together. It was these times when Satori felt a connection to Sarah, less of a mother and daughter and more of a human to human. They enjoyed it so much it was almost their own little tradition. So, even though it is not yet the weekend, Satori allowed the intrusion on her sleepiness. Neither of them had anywhere to be before Monday.

Before long, Sarah reminded her mom it was their Christmas Morning. They agreed when they came home, they would start making their own traditions and treat this morning like Christmas. A new Christmas. A happy, just the two of them Christmas day. Satori knew it would not be much different from their long-standing tradition. There would be just one major change. Joyce. Now Satori would be the one playing Matron and Sarah would be the one playing daughter. That would be very different.

Sarah wanted her mom to open the gift she made first. Another tradition in the Stone family was to make each other presents. Santa gave the purchased presents, and they gave each other handmade. Satori especially loved this part of their traditions. She cherished how much love Sarah put into the gifts she makes. The more rudimentary the better. Last year she gave her mom a teddy bear she made. All from her own pattern. The face was even sewn on by hand. It was adorable, and Satori took it with her whenever she had a business trip.

This year Satori made her daughter a new quilt. Her baby quilt was about to fall to pieces because she still insists on sleeping with it every night. Satori couldn't wait any longer for her to see it. It had all of her favorite things: Frogs, skulls, and aliens; and in all her favorite colors: green, orange, and purple. So, the girls got up and headed to the living room. Sarah plugged in the imitation Christmas tree they decorated before they left. It was so bright and cheery. All the ornaments and lights were white, gold, or silver. Satori headed into the kitchen to make the traditional cinnamon rolls, bacon, and orange juice breakfast. The second time in as many weeks they had this breakfast. About thirty minutes later they sat down to open the gifts. Sarah insisted her mom open her present first. It just might be Sarah enjoys giving gifts more than getting them. Just maybe.

Sarah was odd in these ways; it is a good kind of odd. She does not have a rebellious bone in her body. Satori hopes it will stay this way as she grows up. Sarah does get a pre-teen tone now and then. Still nothing over the top. Sarah even tells Satori she appreciates the rules and limits she is given. Sarah says it helps her feel loved and cared for. Sarah is older than her years would indicate. It makes Satori wonder how she could have been blessed with such a gift, an angel. Then she remembers what her mom Joyce always said in her journals. "You are such a blessing, my gift."

Satori suddenly realized, every time she said this, she was telling her in her own way, the secret she had kept for all these years. Satori literally was a gift, wrapped in a blanket, in a basket. She wasn't just being metaphorical, in the way Satori or other mothers are when they say you are such a gift or a blessing, she meant it.

It's then Satori knew without a doubt her mother can claim her. Joyce might not have birthed Satori, but she loved and cared for her in every way a mother does. Right then, looking at the light in her own daughter's eyes Satori forgave her mom for keeping this secret. Joyce could not have handled the disappointment in Satori's eyes. Joyce did the best she could with what she had. Moreover, she loved Satori, without question. So, Satori said a little prayer to her and sent her love. A warm breeze crossed Satori's cheek, and she clasped her hand to face knowing her mother heard.

Satori opened her daughter's present and her eyes welled with emotion. The same thing happens every time she gets a handmade gift from Sarah. This year Sarah made a clay heart and painted it to look like Satori's stone. The heart shaped rock had been with her as long as she could remember, she had not known for sure where or when it was from she just knew it had always been there. How fitting she thought Sara made her a gift of the stone for

Christmas. The original stone was labradorite about the size of the palm of her hand. She loved looking at it and rolling it around in the light. It had flecks and streaks of bright colored sections; blues, yellows, greens even purples and pinks in some places. It varied from black to gray but was mostly black, and sometimes you could see these iridescent elements.

Loving those rare iridescent parts is exactly why she gave Sarah the middle name of Iridess. Growing up, her mother would say, it's your traveling companion. Never really elaborating and dodging any questions about where Joyce had gotten it. Satori now remembered Joyce telling her one day, "You just showed up with it one day." Satori always thought she meant she came home from school with it, or found it while riding her bike and didn't remember how. Now she knew this rock was in the basket with her when she was found. She could not help but admire Joyce's maneuvering to tell her the truth while still never telling her a truth or a lie. This gem and the "Satori" journal of student publications are all Satori had for clues as to who she really was.

Satori knew Sarah understood how much she treasured her labradorite heart stone. Sarah could not have known what a pivotal role it was playing in her Christmas this year. This made Satori's eyes well-up even more. Satori adored the gift and from her reaction, Sarah thought she had really hit it out of the park with this one. She was so proud of herself.

Sarah was high on enthusiasm when it was time to open her gift from her mom, she squealed with excitement. Opening the box, she wasn't sure at first what it was but knew immediately she loved the fabrics. Sarah pulled it out and saw all her favorite things and colors. Then she turned the quilt over to see it was backed with soft fluffy fur and peeking through in shapes of stars was fuzzy mustache material. Mustaches were the new craze for tweens and teens alike. Hipsters and pointy mustaches had made a comeback. You could find them everywhere.

Sarah loved the quilt. She quizzed Satori for at least ten minutes on how she managed to hide making it when Sarah was in her craft room all the time. Satori explained it hadn't been easy. Sarah grabbed the last present from under the tree and they left to go see Naoma next door.

Naoma opened the door as the girls reached the edge of her driveway yelling, "It's about time you came over to see me!"

Naoma welcomed them in and whispered as Satori went by, "You didn't call me like you said you would." Satori wondered how she knew. Then again this is Naoma we are talking about. She pretty much knew everything; she had the best intuition of anyone Satori ever knew. Satori did say she would call, but how did she explain this thing she was still trying to understand herself. Naoma just nodded her head up and down and said, "You will realize one day I know more than you think I do."

They opened their gifts for each other and Naoma put on a pot of coffee. Naoma was the first to broach the subject, "Sarah, your mom and I need to talk with you." Satori looked at Naoma in shock. It really was uncanny how she did these things. Satori assumed there was no explanation needed for Naoma.

Sarah was only casually interested and said, "Yeah, so what's up." Acting as though her world wasn't about to be destroyed she continued, "You need to talk to me because you can't stand how jealous you are of my iPad. You want to set up a shared custody program or something? Well, the answer is no. Get your own!" and she giggled as little girls do who think they just said the funniest thing ever heard.

They all laughed. Mostly at Sarah rather than with her, but Sarah really didn't care why as long as everyone was laughing.

After the laughter died down Satori decided there was no time like the present and she got started. She explained Grandma Joyce had left a journal for her to find. Satori explained she was really wasn't sure what to make of it all and, so she didn't say anything while they were in Winona.

"Oh my god, Mom, you're scaring me. What is going on?" Sarah bounced uncomfortably on the cushion.

"I am getting to it," Satori retorted. "If you would give me a chance." She fidgeted with her hands around her face not knowing where to put them.

"Yeah, so what did grandma say?" Sarah motioned in fast circles with her hands letting her mom know to move it along.

"She told me the story of my birth, and it was different than I had known before." Satori was having a hard time with eye contact let alone finding the right words.

"What do you mean, different than what you had known before? Like you had a twin who died or something, or wait no, you were born a boy and they made you girl." Sarah joked. "Ewww, Mom you are really a boy!"

Smiling, Satori responded, "No sweetheart. You know how when grandma always said I was the best gift she was ever given, kind of like I tell you."

"Yeah." Sarah squinted inquisitively.

"Well, when grandma said it, she was being literal. Meaning, I was given to her. Or, she found me rather. As an infant. At the top of the stairs at one of the buildings on campus. Which means she is isn't really my mom, someone else is. Someone we don't know or even know how to find." Satori sighed and her shoulders feel with tension she didn't even realize she had been holding.

Rolling her eyes, Sarah said, "So, that's what you've been worried about all week." pausing waiting for more, "that's really it?"

"That's it?" Satori retorted with surprise.

"Yeah. I mean, big deal. So, you don't have her blood. It doesn't mean she isn't your mom. She raised you, she loved you, she was there for you when you scraped your knee or needed money for school. She was the one who was around, the other lady wasn't, whoever she is." Sarah continued. "I mean it's just like Naoma and me. She is always here for me when you can't be. She doesn't have my blood, but she loves me and takes care of me just like a real grandma would."

Satori was in awe. A little hurt, a little beside herself, but still in awe. She had no clue how this mini-human-being had the forethought at twelve to understand better than she does at thirty-seven.

Satori looked at her and wondered aloud, "So then, you're okay with this. Your world hasn't been turned upside down?"

With a know-it-all preteen face, Sarah spurted out, "No."

Satori felt this was all a little anticlimactic. Teenagers, you can never predict when they are going to decide to pull out their inner diva.

The girls stayed at Naoma's a little longer and Satori told them everything she had learned reading the journals. Naoma indicated she might be able to help with the search. Satori felt like it was an impossible undertaking but welcomed the help.

Naoma then told Satori she had a feeling more happened than Satori was letting on. Satori said, "You mean the guy I met on the airplane?" trying and failing to hide the excitement in her voice.

"A guy? I didn't know you met a guy, Mom." Sarah piped in.

"Yeah, we are going on a date Saturday night." Satori eagerly shared

"No." Naoma stated clearly ignoring the eagerness in Satori's tone wanting to talk about her possible romantic interlude.

Naoma went on to explain a date was decidedly — not— what she felt; Naoma said there was danger around Satori. There was something dark looming in her aura. Naoma said she felt it was tied to Winona, like Satori had been watched. Satori suddenly remembered her paranoia about the car she kept seeing.

Satori told Naoma about the blue Impala and Naoma confirmed this is what she was sensing. She said the energy from this car intended to do Satori harm.

Satori got chills down her spine and her skin prickled. She thought she was just being paranoid. Now she was worried she hadn't been paranoid enough. What if something had happened to her or worse, to Sarah.

Naoma asked Satori all kinds of questions trying to

see if she had seen the person's face or could remember any details. Satori was really starting to freak out. Naoma tried to reassure her the issue was in Winona not Wichita and she shouldn't worry. Naoma also assured Satori she would work on both issues; finding Satori's real parents and finding out why there had been a dark cloud following her.

Naoma was odd in this way. She never said how she did things; she just did them, almost like magic. Satori would tell her she really needed to get an oil change and the next day Naoma would bring her a coupon for a free oil change and tire rotation. It would accompany some story about how she found it on the ground or in a coffee shop, but Satori wondered if she didn't really just go buy it to help her out. Naoma was such a giving person. Still, Satori was not sure how Naoma was going to buy her a set of parents or an anti-dark cloud machine. But she decided to leave it to Naoma.

9 Spread Your Wings and Fly

There was nothing more to be done with the dark cloud but there was still the issue of the date and as Saturday night approached Satori began to remember what it was like to feel butterflies in her belly. It had been far longer than she would care to admit since she had been on a date. It wasn't as if she didn't want to date, Satori just never made the time to pursue dating. She filled her time with work and her daughter. Still she saw no reason to look a gift horse in the mouth, or this case a demi-god of a man who for some reason wanted to date her.

Sarah on the other hand was having a much more challenging time adjusting to the change. Sarah hadn't known her mom to date. Not even once. So, while Naoma had agreed Sarah could stay with her for the night, Sarah wasn't as keen on the idea. Sarah didn't understand why she couldn't go along. Sarah argued, she and Satori were a package deal to get one was to get them both; therefore, the date should include them both. Satori agreed if the relationship grew it would definitely need to include Sarah, but she tried to explain how in the beginning she needed to see if this was someone she wanted around longer than a date or two. And for this she needed to be on her own. Besides, she didn't want to string a long line of guys in and out of Sarah's life.

Sarah just rolled her eyes and said, "Yeah, because there has been such a huge line of guys at our door so far, Mom."

Exasperated with trying to use logic Satori resorted to bargaining and bribery. She promised Sarah to take her to dinner at Sarah's favorite restaurant next week. Being a single mom Satori had to stick to a very strict budget, but it had been a while since they splurged, even while they were in Winona, they stayed on a tight budget. Satori figured this one time could not do much damage.

Darvey called Friday to confirm the time and get Satori's address. He insisted on being a true gentleman. He was picking her up at her house. She did not remember much about dating, but what she did remember was these days guys usually don't bother picking you up. You met somewhere neutral and in public. Dutch all the way. Partly for safety and partly because chivalry was dead, the saying was not just a clever pun. Satori however adored chivalry and did not fear for her safety with Naoma next door. She doubted much would occur with Sarah and Naoma peeking through a slap in the mini-blinds on the front door. Sarah was clueless as to who it was Satori was talking about from the flight having been half-asleep or engrossed in her iPad the entire time. To add insult to injury neither one believed Satori's description of the adonis slash god slash man hunk. First, they did not believe someone so attractive was actually real enough to live in the middle of nowhere Kansas. Second, how was that same someone traveling from Winona at the exact same time? Third, why would someone sit and listen to the drone of a boring life for hours? Then, after all this, that very same person would actually ask a comparatively plain jane on a date. It sounded too dreadful, too unlikely, too one-in-a-million to be true. No. There was absolutely zero chance any of this was true. In fact, Satori started to wonder if it was all a dream herself. Would she be alone? Would Darvey show up to her house or had she imagined the entire thing?

It wasn't all a dream however, it was all true and real and perfect. Darvey was annoyingly perfect in almost every way. In so many ways one might not even notice the ways in which he isn't. Or wasn't as it were. But then, we are jumping ahead of ourselves again. The story really is so much better when we unwind it slowly and carefully; just as it was unwound for Satori herself.

Saturday night arrived, as did Darvey, right on time, in fact three minutes early. Satori appreciated a punctual person. She was a bit OCD when it comes to things being in order. Being on time falls right in line with her obsession with perfection. As it turns out, the perfection of Darvey Lavender fell right in line with her obsession as well. He pulled into the driveway and got out of the car with a bouquet of Calla Lilies. Satori wondered how he knew they were her favorite.

Satori welcomed Darvey in and asked him to make himself at home while she put the flowers in water. Darvey walked over to the fireplace to look at some of the decorations and knickknacks on display. Satori went in the kitchen to get a vase and fresh cut the stems. Turning on the faucet, she placed the ends of the stems in the sink and reached to the top of the refrigerator for the vase. Even on her tiptoes she was finding it difficult to reach. It must have been pushed back somehow. Satori was going to have to go get her stepladder.

Seeing the predicament, Darvey quickly came to her rescue. He came into the kitchen and made his way behind Satori. So as not to startle her he placed the palm of his left hand in the small of her back and reached over her to grab the vase with his right hand. The motion pushed his chest into her back and her chest into the refrigerator. Satori's breath caught, and she was frozen with his touch and his smell lingering on her gently. She remembered his smell now and wondered how it was she could have forgotten. The delicious manly rugged smell mixed with masculine cologne. The electricity was still there between them as well, just as it had been on the flight. Only now it was not just in their fingers but throughout their entire bodies. This closeness was comfortable and energizing. Satori hadn't realized she missed it as much as she did. She would have been happy to stay right there the entire night and not move an inch. Realizing this might get awkward. She cleared her throat. Which is where she realized she wasn't the only one who had been wrapped up in the moment and Darvey had been taking her in as well. They both flushed.

Satori thanked him for his help and tried to unfreeze herself. Darvey asked for her kitchen shears, so she opened the drawer by the fridge and handed them to him.

Darvey went to the sink and placed the vase under the running water. Taking the shears, he placed each stem under the running water and pruned the end at a diagonal. Then placed it into the vase filling with water. He was careful and gentle. Satori admired him for knowing how to properly fill a vase with fresh flowers. When he was finished, he put the vase in the opening between the kitchen and the living room and asked if the placement was okay. Satori nodded wondering again, how he knew exactly where she always put her fresh flowers. Maybe the placement was just the most obvious location, perfectly situated between the living room and the kitchen. Seen by almost all the front rooms equally.

Darvey reached out his hand in a gesture indicating an opening. Satori moved toward him, and he placed his hand in the small of her back again. She loved the feeling of a man's hand in the small of her back. They went around the dining room and into the living room. Darvey picked up Satori's coat up off the edge of the sofa where she laid it while getting ready. Helping her into her jacket Darvey asked if she was ready to go.

Satori was smitten. She wondered, "Who is this guy? He has manners, he is gorgeous, and he obviously thinks I am decent looking as well." She was really struggling to find a flaw in him. Then she remembered, he is too good to be true. This of course by default meant she is going to mess this up. A constant stream of expletives started playing through her head. She finally decided she might as well just tell him to be on his way now. It was better to save the heartache.

Darvey narrowing his eyes and wondering where she had gone in her head tried getting her attention, "Satori, are you okay?"

Satori took a deep breathy sigh, "Yeah, I'm fine. I'm just sure I am going to screw this up. I'm wondering if we should even go. I mean the last thing I need is get my heart broken by the last decent man on earth. Sorry, I know there is nothing like changing my mind at the last minute."

He just gave her his half-cocked smile and said, "Well, I am not sure about heartbreak, it's just dinner. And I'm not even sure if I'm a decent man. But I will tell you this much, you will have to work hard to mess this up. I have a story to tell you over dinner." Then with a little more sternness to his voice, "And we are going to dinner. So, let's get going."

Satori smiled at him and thought, "Yep, heartbreak is a certainty. Fantastic job, Satori. You're really going to wrench this one up."

The drive to the restaurant was pleasant. Darvey and Satori talked about insignificant things like weather and construction on the highway across town, which neither of them had ever seen without orange cones as long as they had lived in Wichita. About ten minutes in, Darvey reached over and put his hand on top of Satori's, which had been resting on her left knee. Satori then knew despite his pulled together demeanor, he was nervous too. Darvey's palms were sweating like it was the middle of summer not the middle of winter. This fact only made Satori more endeared toward him. The Demi-god was human after all. Not only was he human, but he was nervous with someone as normal and plain as she was.

His gesture seemed to put them both a little more at ease and by the time they reached Red Rock Canyon Grill their fingers had found their way in between each other. Satori was in heaven, well heaven on earth anyway. They found a parking spot right next to the front door. As they pulled in Darvey asked Satori to wait for him to get out and open her door.

As she waited in the car she thought how much she was enjoying all this gentlemanly behavior. It was refreshing and honestly, she had not experienced it before in her life with any man she had dated. As a single mom, she was always so proud of her independence and ability to accomplish everything on her own. Still, she had to admit it was refreshing to be treated so well. She felt it was safe to take off her armor for a night and let someone else play protector. She had always assumed letting someone else lead or be in charge would feel stifling or lessening in some way. She was finding it did not. There was absolutely no insult in allowing someone to open a door for her. Satori thought more than anything it felt respectful. After all, he knew her life story from the plane ride to Denver; he knew darn good and well she could open a door. Darvey opening it for her was like he was saying, I know you can, but let me have some of your load, I can help. Satori already adored this man, his heart, his human, who he was aside from his body and his face.

Darvey opened Satori's door and put out his hand to help her up. Then shut the door behind her and offered his elbow for her to hold.

As they walked in the hostess seemed to be

waiting for them. Satori thought this was unusual because even with a reservation, at Red Rock on a Saturday night, everyone waits. In fact, there were people waiting on this Saturday. The hostess welcomed Darvey immediately. "Welcome Mr. Lavender, it is wonderful to see you again. We have your table waiting if you would please follow me."

Suddenly, Satori knew, she figured out what was going on. Darvey Lavender was a player, and she was his next plaything. She started boiling inside wondering why she had not seen it sooner. She thought, the entire over-the-top romantic gestures, the flowers, the opening doors... Why in the world would a guy this gorgeous want anything to do with a girl like her, so plain and normal? Why else would this hostess know him by sight and name, and have his table ready and waiting with all these other people ahead of them? She was so happy to see him again and wasn't surprised he was with a woman she had never seen him with before. This must be his go-to first date location. She should have known from the second she saw him. Men that good looking with smiles that wry don't get that way with no history. He must have women at his feet. Satori was steaming inside.

She decided right then, she was not going to be another one of Darvey's conquests. He was going to buy her dinner, and not an "Oh, he he he he, I'm just a tiny little girl who eats salad." kind of dinner either. Satori was getting a big dinner, whatever was most expensive, maybe two. The kind where he is going to wonder where it all fit. Satori couldn't believe she had been falling for it. And she had been falling. Every single look, glance, and smile, hook, line, and sinker.

She was buying every bit of it like Darvey meant it.

They sat down, Darvey holding Satori's chair for her before seating himself across from her. Darvey noticed Satori's changed demeanor. He asked if the table location was alright or if she would prefer to sit somewhere else? Satori shook her head and looked down at the table.

She couldn't hold it in any longer. The only thing less controlled than her paranoia was her ability to keep her emotions in check. So, of course, she decided to pull the wrench out. Because, well, why not? She looked up and began to verbally vomit all over his plans of making her his next conquest.

She held her head high, took a deep breath and started, "It's nice to see you AGAIN, Mr. Lavender." Eyes like slits aiming at their pray. "I mean if you were just going to try to schmooze your way into my pants you are sorely mistaken. What kind of girl do you think I am?" Her hands had joined her one woman circus. "I have some self-respect. The least you could have done is bring me someplace where you don't take all your other dates." She at least had the decency not to make a scene and was keeping her voice lowered. It was the only shred of humility she had hung on to as her heart beat in her chest with anger and disgust.

Darvey got a crooked silly grin on his face, almost as if he was going to laugh at Satori, which only served to make her want to toss the wrench she was welding straight in his face. He wiped his face with his napkin. Asked if she was finished and if he could please be given the opportunity to defend his honor. He looked around and found a waiter, motioning for him to come over; he put his hand on Satori's in an attempt to calm her. She recoiled, still not wanting to make too much of a scene, she pulled her hand slowly away rather than with the quickness she wanted.

Darvey asked the waiter to please see if the hostess could come over for a moment.

Darvey focusing his attention back on Satori now said, "I did say it would difficult to mess this up Satori. I didn't say it would be impossible. I understand how it could have looked but please give me a little a credit. I am a good guy. You will learn this about me if you give me a chance to show you." Satori returned her attention to the table because the hostess was returning. Satori wasn't sure what to expect. A grand lie or utter embarrassment, but either way she braced herself for a quick exit.

Darvey thanked her for coming back and said, "I am hoping you could clear something up for me."

"Absolutely, Mr. Lavender," she chirped.

"When was the last time you saw me in here?" Darvey asked.

She replied, "It has been a while Mr. Lavender. I think it has been almost two years. Yes, two years because I had just started dating Jon, you remember Jon don't you? "

Satori's eyes widened. She didn't expect that. How could he be so familiar with this girl yes have not seen her for two years? This was all very confusing she thought.

"Yes, of course, the football player. I hope you two are doing well."

She began to inundate Darvey with the details of their romance and Darvey appeared to be very caring. It made Satori even more curious about the man with which she was having dinner.

When she finished Darvey thanked her and said he

wouldn't keep her any longer.

Darvey explained he used to bring his mother here every week for a date night. It was her favorite restaurant. She had been diagnosed with breast cancer. Just like Satori's mother, and similar to Joyce, rather than fighting she decided to live her life without treatment. So, every Saturday night while she was able Darvey would bring his mother here to her favorite restaurant. She had passed away almost 2 years ago now, and he had not been back since.

He also said they developed a close relationship with some employees, Kylee being one of them. His mother never had a daughter of her own and so had become very fond of Kylee. When she passed, she left the young girl a substantial amount of money for college. This is why she remembered Darvey so well, and not because he regularly came in with girls.

He went on to explain when Satori was telling him her story on the plane about so recently losing her own mother in much the same way, he felt drawn to her. He had wished for someone who could understand what he had been through and what he had lost. So, when Satori agreed to go on a date with him, he also knew where he should bring her. He called ahead and spoke and with Kylee asking to make sure his table was available because he was bringing in a special date for dinner. Calla Lilies were his mother's favorite flower, this is why he brought those to her tonight. He would always bring her a fresh bouquet each week when he picked her up, he would cut them and put them in the vase over her kitchen sink. He needed his mother's memory to give him strength to make it through this night. He hadn't dated in a long time and he felt his mother Satori to him.

This was the point Satori started to feel like a complete ass. Here she was thinking he was male a pig, and he was truly a sweet kind caring man who lost his mom and missed her terribly. Just because he was gorgeous didn't mean he slept with every woman he could find. She felt so ashamed for judging him so harshly and wondered if he would even still be willing to continue after the way she behaved so far. She had been a complete loon. Any guy in their right mind would run.

So, she did what any self-respecting loon would do in the same situation. Stuck her head in the sand. Which in this case meant hung her head and thought about how awful she was? It turns out the wrench she thought she had flung at Darvey was really boomeranging right back in her own face.

"Satori, are you okay?" Darvey asked.

When she finally looked up, she had a tear in her eye. "I am so sorry for assuming the worst; I completely understand if you want to just take me home now, or even call me a cab'" she explained.

He started laughing. Satori was dumbfounded.

"You have so much spunk and fire in you, Satori. Why would I want to send you home in a cab? I haven't even schmoozed my way into your pants yet," he said with a giggle.

Confused and slightly amused, Satori smirked and cocked her head at him.

"Look, you had no way of knowing about my mom. It's adorable how you have the guts to stick up for yourself. You go weak in the knees whenever I am close to you. Do you have any idea what that does to a guy's ego?" he asked. "I feel like I have won first place at the county fair and you're my blue ribbon."

"I'm your ribbon?" Satori pondered.

"Yes. Mom and I would sit in this very booth for hours talking about what I was going to do with my life when she was gone. She wanted desperately for me to find a good woman, settle down, and raise a family. I told her I was too old for a family, and I was too young for a good woman. I told her all my do's and don'ts for my perfect girl. She said when she died, she was going to make it her mission to put the girl I wanted in my path. She said just to make sure I knew it was the right one, I would find her on an airplane. So, there could be no mistaking. When we met on an airplane she was the right girl for me."

Satori just stared at him.

"She asked what color eyes I wanted her to have. To which I replied, "Are you sure you want to get so specific, what if you can't find her Mom?" She told me the more specific the better and leave finding the girl up to her. So, I said, "Well, blue I guess, then I changed it to green, and jokingly I said heck why not yellow. We laughed a bit, and I said, I tell you what, give her any of those colors or all of those colors. And if it all three, I will have no doubt and when I want to walk away like I always do, I will know, she is the one, and I am supposed to stay. I didn't expect her to send me anyone. Well, I guess part of me did. But I didn't expect to meet anyone with all three colors in their eyes either." Darvey explained.

"That is why when you were talking on the flight all I could do was stare at your eyes. Seriously, Satori, who has eyes like yours? Blue, green, and yellow? You can't scare me away."

Satori was at a loss and didn't know what to say.

She recalled sitting in her bed many months ago, maybe even years at this point, and writing out a list of what her perfect man should be. She tried remembering which of her journals it was in. What had she written on those pages? How much of it was Darvey she wondered? Did his mother really find her and bring them together? It isn't like she looked very far; they had both been in Wichita after all. Satori wasn't sure she really believed in what Darvey was saying but she was thankful for one thing, Darvey believed it. And if he believed it he was going to put up with her behaving in such unbecoming ways and still be interested in her.

This got her wondering a little more. Was this the only reason he was still with her now? What happened when the allure of her eye color wasn't enough to keep him interested any longer? Would she be enough to keep him around? Because Satori still couldn't see herself as Darvey saw her, a radiantly beautiful woman. One who was kind, if not honest to a fault? Brave yet timid. Spending time with Satori was an easy task for Darvey one he was more than happy to oblige.

He reached across the table and put his hand out. Satori reached back toward him. As their fingers touched, the sparks were there again. Bright and alive. They were both growing used to the connection they had. Growing used to the not so silent universe nudging their souls together. They intertwined their fingers and looked into each other's eyes. Then in unison, they said, "Okay," smiling. "Okay."

This was Satori's first time at the Red Rock; she didn't venture much to the east side of town. But she enjoyed it very much. Darvey, knowing she hadn't been there before asked what she usually liked to eat, and then offered to order for her. They did something with their dinner salad it melted in your mouth. Maybe it was the Ranchero dressing, or the cornbread croutons, or the candied pecans, but Satori had never had anything like it. She was in love. With the salad at least. Then Darvey ordered her something called a Cluck and Moo which was far too much to eat, but was delicious. You could watch the rotisserie chickens being cooked and the steak was amazingly perfect melt in your mouth scrumptious.

When dinner was over they both looked grief stricken, their conversation had come easily, and they discovered they had so much in common. Satori knew Sarah would be worried and she should get home. Still, she wanted to spend more time with Darvey. There wasn't much use in pretending, they both knew this thing between them was happening. They had a moment. Unless one found a way to irritate the other, they were in this. There weren't those awkward questions of how well does he like me or does she like me. It was just clear. They each were so enamored.

As Darvey drove Satori home they held hands, reaching over into Satori lap. As they neared the west side, and the stoplights started becoming frequent Darvey was anticipating the drop off and everything that implies. While he and Satori had been connecting, if not igniting, at an unparalleled pace, the first kiss is always filled with anxious anticipation. He hoped to help calm her nerves a bit and his. At the next yellow, he stopped even though he could have pushed through.

Darvey turned toward Satori and smiled at her. Even though he remembered the way to her house, he asked which street he was supposed to turn down. After she answered, "Just past the light on the right at Murray and then an immediate left."

"Thank you" and he carefully lifted her hand to his mouth turning her hand back-side up. Gently and softly his lips met her skin lingering just long enough for Satori to flush with the realization she was about to make out with a demi-god. At that moment they also both realized the electricity in their touch magnified in their lips. A chill leaped though Satori's whole body. Darvey returned her hand to her lap and Satori circled her thumb over his wondering how they had fallen so easily in step with each other. Darvey pulled into the driveway and Satori guided him to the space on the far right side. It was the least likely location for peeping from Naoma's house she imagined.

"I would invite you in, but I am sure Sarah and Naoma are watching us right now. I'm not sure she is ready to see me bring a man into the house."

He nodded his head in understanding and stretched to see if he could see any of the windows from the neighbor's house. "I understand. Although it doesn't seem they can see us here." After a pause, "I have had a wonderful time with you tonight, I mean, after you stopped thinking you were the date of the week." Darvey's familiar cocked grin took over Satori and she was drowning him. They both chuckled. Satori's laugh was a little woozier than she had felt a couple minutes before.

Darvey wondered, "What do you think Sarah would say if we just had a small kiss? Honestly, I have been thinking about kissing you since the airplane. I almost kissed you then just to get you to be quiet for a minute." And he smiled a devilish grin.

"I wish you would have, I was mortified when I realized I just kept talking the entire time," Satori smiled sheepishly and coy "And, well, to be honest, there are worse things than being kissed by a handsome stranger."

"We aren't strangers anymore…" he said with over the top romantic undertones and a quirk in his lip.

Satori grinned while deciding if sticking her finger down her throat in mock horror of his attempt to be romantic was going too far.

"We aren't on a flight either. And I am just going to sit here in awkward silence until you get up the courage to kiss me already."

This only made Darvey even more nervous than he had been before. He was used to being in charge and this somehow took him off his footing. The truth is Satori was scared to death of being kissed by a god. But this god was just as scared to kiss her. So, they both sat there with their aura's vibrating nervously next to each other. Transferring their energy back and forth. Digging into his guts, Darvey found his courage and pulled it up into his throat.

He leaned forward placing his fingers on her left cheek and his palm at her chin and said, "Satori Stone, you pierce me."

Closing his eyes and leaning forward the electricity started to build between them. It was almost audible. The delicate hairs on Satori's face began to twitch in reaction. It was exactly like what they experienced when the shook hands only more intimate. They were both in awe at the sensations they were feeling. The anticipation was building and the wonder of kissing, once they actually touched. Darvey slowed his approach to ensure they could both feel what was happening and know if they were really feeling it. They were in awe at the sensation and as much as they wanted to kiss neither wanted the feeling to end either.

Darvey whispered, "Do you feel that?"

Satori nodded slightly barely moving her head and inhaled deeply. She smelled it again. Him. Darvey. His woodsy, musky, smell like man and myth. Her head was swooning.

Closer.

They were millimeters apart.

Closer.

The kiss was coming.

Closer.

Instinct was taking over and the awe of the electricity was wearing off, they needed to feel each other's lips. To taste each other's breath.

Closer.

BEEP BEEP BEEP BEEP

Darvey's car horn started blaring in their ears.

Jumping apart like teenagers who's dad just flipped on the lights in the basement.

"What the hell?" came out in unison.

Reaching in his pocket Darvey pulled out the key fob to his white Porsche Cayenne. Realizing at the same time it had been in his pocket and the panic button pushed up against the seatbelt as he leaned toward Satori.

Satori began to flush red as lights in the neighborhood began turning on from house to house. Moments later, Naoma's porch light was on as well.

"I guess we have been caught," Darvey lamented.

Smiling, Satori leaned over and gave him a peck on the check, "Another time, Mr. Lavender!"

"Another time then, Ms. Stone." And a heavy sigh escaped him.

Getting out, Darvey came around to the passenger side to open Satori's door for her. Holding hands, they walked to the front door. It was a bone chilling wintry night out, so Darvey quickly made sure she was able to get in the house, kissed Satori's forehead, smiled, looked into her eyes full of regret and want and went back to his car.

Satori stood at the storm door and waved goodbye as he drove away. Wishing more than anything, she would have had the courage and gumption to invite him in, propriety be damned. She took in a deep breath then suddenly realizing this breath she took no longer smelled like Darvey at all, she closed her eyes and sighed. Putting her left overs in the fridge she went to her bedroom, took a shower and found her pillow. Feeling more at ease than she had been in a long time. Even if more than a little wistful.

10 Too Good To Be True

The next several weeks seemed to fly by. They were filled with butterflies and promises of beginnings without endings. Darvey and Satori went on several more dates. Not only dinner and the movies but they took in some culture with the Final Friday Art and Trolley Tour in downtown Wichita. There was even a night when Sarah had a sleep-over at Alexis's house. This is when things really started heating up between them. Things had been on the edge of smoldering the whole time they were dating; but, the opportunity had not presented itself to take their relationship to the next level.

Darvey invited Satori over to his place to start the evening. While normally he would prefer picking her up, they both knew where this night was expected to go. It seemed like as good of a night as any for Satori to familiarize herself with his home.

She followed Siri down Commerce Street to an old warehouse pulling in between and behind the buildings as Darvey had explained. Easily finding a parking space, she exited her car and walked around to the front of the building. She buzzed the doorbell, and it rang back to her as the door unlatched allowing her into the elevator. She pressed the button for the third floor and pulled the old heavy cargo gate closed. The car lurched to a start alarming Satori. She knew the building was old but somehow had expected it to be more greased or smooth. Instead, it was jerky and heavy and made her wonder if she was safe to ride at all.

It slowly creaked to a stop on the third floor and she pulled open the heavy gate again and knocked on Darvey's door. There was no hallway, so Satori surmised he had the entire level to himself. Having heard the beast of an elevator making its way up the shaft Darvey was already at the door and opening it before she finished knocking.

"Come on in," he smiled kissing her on the forehead and reaching out to take her jacket and purse.

From outside the building and then the elevator Satori half expected they would be sitting on milk crates and his clothes would be hanging from meat hooks. However, when she walked in she received a shock. Her breath was taken away as she inhaled the expanse of the interior with its high ceilings, the modern and luxurious finishes were perfectly balanced with the rustic floors and original brick walls. Still, the surface had been polished somehow. In a way which kept the rustic nature while at the same time allowing the wood and stone to look brand new. From the entrance you could see the entire loft. It was spacious and expansive. While predominantly void of walls there were clear designations and functions within the space. Directly in front of her was a beautiful dining table with an Edison bulb chandelier hanging above it. Beyond the dining table in the corner was a chef-worthy appointed kitchen with an island. To the left was the living and room and what appeared to be a library or study area with books and shelves and cozy seating surfaces. Then there was

Darvey's bed, which created the impression she was going to need a stepladder to get into. And no matter what, she was going to be getting into it. In the final corner, out in the open was a glass enclosed rain shower, a claw foot bath tub and what she assumed was the rest of a bathroom behind one of the few walls in the flat. It was manly yet not so overdone a woman wouldn't be comfortable. It was modern and still comfortable. It was well appointed and tasteful and clearly put together by someone who had the money to make sure no expense was spared even while not being overly flashy. Seeing his place she was a bit embarrassed at letting him over to her house all these times, she must seem so quaint compared to what he was used to.

Darvey had made some hors d'oeuvre for them, not the lil'smokies wrapped in croissant rolls as Satori made, but real honest canapés. He also had her favorite drink waiting for her. Disaronno on the rocks. He handed her the drink and kissed her lips after her first sip, licking his lips from the sweet residue. As everything in Darvey's fashion seemed, nothing about him was ordinary. The ice cube in her drink was a perfectly frozen ball and pivoted around a cone shaped bevel in the center of her glass. It seemed to make the amaretto taste even more perfect.

They decided to start their night with dinner and a movie. They made their way down Santa Fe and later continued over to Mead until they reached Old Town Square where the Warren Movie Theater was located. They already knew they wanted to watch Hansel and Gretel: Witch Hunters so Darvey had preordered the tickets. This was one of those theaters where you can order dinner and drinks and they bring them right to your own personal reclining seat. Satori was so nervous she barely touched her salad and fries. It wasn't every day you anticipate an evening with a god, naked and sweaty. They sat in the back of the theater and by the time the second preview had begun anyone who had seen them would have mistaken them for teenagers not the thirty-somethings they were. It was as ridiculous as it was fun Satori thought. The freedom of not having to adult even if only for the length of one movie. It had been an unseasonably warm day for January reaching into the seventies, so it was natural after the movie rather than walking straight back to Darvey's loft they hung around the square talking and people watching. While Satori was excited for what came next, she was also very nervous.

Their evening was everything they hoped for and they were both happily sleep deprived. By the time morning arrived, all her nerves were dissolved along with any hesitation. This man was someone she wanted to spend every minute with. She could not believe how fast everything was moving, but she did not want it to slow down either. She had not felt this happy with a man, well, ever.

Darvey, except for the make out session the previous night, hadn't lost his gentlemanly demeanor. He opened every door, stood when she left the table and let Satori take the lead on how fast the relationship moved. One night she arrived home after work to find the snow had been shoveled from her driveway and walkway. Not only at her house but for Naoma's house as well. He left a note on the door which read,

I COULDN'T STAND THE THOUGHT OF YOU IN HARM'S WAY.
MR. LAVENDER

Satori was smitten. There was no question. She was in awe that this man found her so special. She was grateful for his mom even though she didn't believe in coincidence and that manifesting stuff. She felt like people usually found what they were looking for because they were looking for it. Not because it was sent to you. Still, Satori wasn't going to turn it away. At the very least Darvey's mom sowed a seed and Satori was all too happy to harvest. Darvey checked every item off Satori's wish list for a guy. So if there was something to this whole manifesting thing, then she was just as likely to have called him into her life as he was to have called her into his. She didn't much care who manifested who, all she knew is Darvey was perfect. More than that, he was utterly and completely wrench free, Satori could see zero tools around him what so ever.

It was almost a month later, on a Monday in February; the 27th. A male voice came from behind her breaking her stream of concentration. She disliked this most about cubicle life; her back was to everyone who entered. She always felt so intruded upon. She was irritated as she looked up from her monitor to roll her eyes at whoever decided they needed her attention without sending a meeting invite. She turned and started, "Yes, What?" with more than a little irritation.

Trailing off as she saw the most beautiful bouquet of flowers. It was in a clear square vase with white calla lilies streaming out to one side. Then up from the center but remaining close to the opening were white hydrangea and several green cymbidium orchids.

With little doubt who they were from, she quickly signed for the flowers and sheepishly handed the delivery boy a $5 bill. Opening the card, she read,

I WANT TO BE A BIGGER PART OF YOUR LIFE, WHEN CAN I MEET YOUR FAMILY?
MR. LAVENDER

Darvey knew, for Satori, her family consisted of Sarah. Sarah was everything. Sarah was a huge step; Sarah was a bigger step even than marriage, really. This was meeting the single most important part of her life. The one thing Satori valued and cherished above all other things.

Then it really dawned on Satori, Darvey knew what this suggested. It must mean she, Satori "Plain Jane" Ariel Stone, meant that much to Darvey "The God" Audric Lavender. Her breath was quickening, and her pulse was running amuck. She sat back in her chair just as her head started spinning away from her. Luckily, her phone rang at the same moment, the nosey receptionist wanted to know if it was her birthday.

There was nothing like a little office gossip to get you firmly planted back in reality.

Satori knew this wasn't just her decision; she was going to have to talk it over with Sarah as well. And she needed to make sure it was something she really wanted to do.

Still, she didn't want to seem ungrateful. So she pulled out her cell and messaged Darvey.

Hey Sexy
Thx 4 the stems. GORG!!!

Instantly Darvey responded.

Just like you, Kitten.

Satori loved how even when she abbreviated everything in text, he would still type everything out like it was an email or an office memo. She also hated how she loved that he called her, Kitten. She wasn't fond of cats in particular. She was more of a dog person. And she felt like she gave up a little, okay a lot of, her femininity to have a pet name like Kitten. Still, it was endearing.

A few minutes later, Darvey messaged again.

What do you think? Are you ready for me to meet your family?

Damn it! Slipped through her lips as she raised her hands to her mouth and looked over her cubicle to see if anyone heard. Luckily if they did hear, no other heads were bothering to bob up and check on the commotion. Sighing with disconnect, she slouched back into her chair and began twirling the loose lock which had wriggled its way out of her bun. She wasn't going to be able to avoid the question after all.

Big step. Talkn w/ Sarah 2nit. Let u know

Setting her phone back on the desk, she felt triumphant. That wasn't as painful as she thought it was going to be.

At least not until her desk vibrated again seconds later letting her know, it wasn't over yet. Damn it! Again!

Darvey replied.

What about Naoma. I am hoping to meet her as well.

Satori's head jumped back in place as she read the last message. She hadn't assumed he meant Naoma when he said family. But then, why wouldn't he? Naoma had been a very big part of her family since her mother passed away. It made sense he would want to meet the two most important people in Satori's life. Satori felt a little guilty a newcomer to her life figured out before she did Naoma was in fact, Satori's family, even if she wasn't related by blood or in any other legal way.

Satori responded.

Oh, ok. Will let u know. Thnx agn Sexy!

Feeling less certain this time she wrapped up the conversation with a pretty bow, she sat the phone back on the desk with the screen face up waiting with bated breath... no pressure... This time no reply came. Success.

Satori could hardly concentrate the rest of the day at work. It's a good thing the flowers were an afternoon delivery. Her knee jumped from her toes to her hip as she tried, unsuccessfully, to concentrate on anything.

She really was a coward when it came to talking about things that actually mattered with the people who mattered most in her life. She much preferred the wait-and-see approach to life. To Satori's surprise both Sarah and Naoma were more than open to meeting Darvey, they were anxious. One more Darvey story without a face to put to it and they were going to burst.

The trio decided they would make dinner at Satori's on Saturday and invite Darvey over. Satori wanted to do all she could to help Sarah ease out of any nerves she might have in meeting a guy her mom was dating. She assumed dinner at home was the perfect setting.

May 3rd arrived quickly, and Satori spent the day re-cleaning all the floors and scrubbing the walls. They didn't need the spit shine, but Satori needed an outlet for her extra energy. Thankfully, Naoma and Sarah were there to help her fix dinner. They planned Sarah's favorite meal, Spaghetti. Not the best dinner if you wanted to keep your clothes clean, but it could be romantic. Just ask Lady and the Tramp. Besides, the goal here was to put Sarah at ease. Except the only person all day who needed help was Satori. She would have given anything for a Lortab or Zanex right about then. As it was, she settled for a double Disaronno on the rocks and then she finally started to calm down.

Darvey pulled into the drive right on time as usual. Satori was setting the last bowl on the table when the doorbell rang. Checking her hair and makeup one last time in the large mirror by the entrance, she made her way to the front door. Naoma and Sarah had been in Sarah's room. Sarah was playing the piano and singing, she loved putting on little shows for anyone who would listen, and Naoma would always listen. They stopped when the doorbell rang and bee lined to the front room.

Taking his jacket and placing it in the front closet, Satori noticed he was a little overdressed for spaghetti in her modest three-bedroom ranch. It sat on a tree-lined street with a stream out front. They called it a stream anyway. It was really just a water run-off from a big ditch the city built to keep everything from flooding when it rained heavily. Kansas was notoriously flat after all and water without direction wreaks havoc on neighborhoods. The stream did offer fun summer past times of catching frogs and tossing in branches to watch them travel downstream. A few brave souls would even launch a raft when the rain was especially high.

While small, the house on Westlink Avenue had a lot of charm. It was built in 1950 and looked like a gingerbread cottage. It even has scalloped eaves and diamond shaped window panels. Right after moving in Satori pulled out all the carpets and refinished the hardwood floors. There was a sun room on the back of the house which was only ever used to listen to the rain. It had a metal roof and made beautiful music when the rain came down. The front bath and Kitchen were still in original condition. It had pink tiles with pink and gray boomerang formica counter tops. You just couldn't find things that cool anymore.

Satori loved her home, but somehow she felt embarrassed at the same time seeing Darvey there dressed so elegantly. He had on casual jeans, cuffed at the bottom, worn brown lace up leather shoes but when it was paired with a yellow long sleeve button up and gray wool V-neck sweater, he was elegantly casual and distinguished. Satori wished she could upgrade her home about five decades with the snap of her fingers.

Still, she loved how he understood what this evening meant to her. How important this evening was, and he didn't just toss on an old t-shirt because they were dining on spaghetti at her house. Satori on the other hand, did just toss something on. Like always, whatever her hand landed on first in the closet. Even for Satori, this still meant she looked elegant and charming, effortlessly. She just had that way. Her style was effortless, but always timeless and elegant. Tonight, it was her favorite peacock blue maxi dress with long flowing sleeves almost as long as the dress. It was cinched at the waist. She threw on a large bangle cuff and a statement necklace, then took off the necklace. She hadn't even bothered with shoes. She thought she needed to be comfortable after all. . The pre-dinner drink had helped to calm her stomach, but she was still wound tight. She leaned in to kiss Darvey hello and he turned his check to her, smiling and nodding to Sarah and Naoma. The amaretto had loosened her up a little too much she thought instantly as warmth brightened her cheeks and body.

"Where are my manners," Satori wondered aloud.

"Darvey, this is my daughter, Sarah. And this is our good friend, Naoma."

Sarah was always true to herself and tonight was no different. She had chosen to wear a pair of light washed blue jeans, tennis shoes, a pink flower skit, a soft pink short-sleeved shirt and her long hair was pinned up in back. Fashion was something Satori and Sarah agreed on completely; and, it is always up to the person who is wearing it. Naoma, on the other hand, was more conservative. She was wearing a dress that once was a splurge to purchase. Naoma never threw anything away, especially not anything this special, even it if was purchased in the 1970s. Naoma, though well-meaning didn't understand some things went out of style. Although given a little more time, it would be back in.

"It's so wonderful to finally meet you," Darvey smiled as he reached out his hand to Sarah and then Naoma.

Satori noticed a puzzled look on Naoma's face. Naoma was not sure about this guy now when she could see him up close. Hoping not to put a damper on the evening, Naoma quickly put a smile back on her face. "Nice to meet you as well, Darvey. Satori has told us so much about you," she responded.

Satori motioned to the table and recommended they all sit down to dinner. The table was set with tea for everyone to drink, cheese melted garlic bread, and enough spaghetti to feed half the city. Still too nervous to eat, Satori took a small portion of spaghetti and nibbled on bread.

The conversation was going smoothly if not with a little interrogating on Naoma's part. Satori thought it was sweet of Naoma to be so concerned. Right up until things got awkward.

Everyone was laughing at one of Sarah's school stories when out of nowhere Naoma turned to Darvey grabbed his hand and pulled it close to her, "This is an interesting ring you have. Where ever did you get something so unique?"

Tensing up and pulling his arm back, Darvey stammered and instinctually, started rubbing the ring on his right ring finger with his thumb. Almost with a glazed over look he said "This old thing. It was given to me by my father. He insisted I always wear it. I guess I don't even realize it is there anymore."

Then, no one said anything. Everyone just stared at his ring.

Darvey's ring was made of white gold. It was circular on top. It had a circle in the middle with horizontal lines through it. Like a plus sign away from the center were four lines each ending with a different symbol, and in between each of these points were additional symbols. The symbols were things Satori had never seen before. Naoma however was very familiar with them. The top of Darvey's ring was one of the Seals of Solomon and known by those-who-knew to be a sign of magic. And not the Houdini "smoke and mirrors" mode of magic or the kind kids read about in magical wizard novels that is all fantasy and fairytale, but real magic. Without some investigation and research, you would not really know if the person practicing the magic was for good or evil. Naoma knew this because she was a mystic. Mystics lived in the world of magic, and they understood it, even better than the so-called magicians. Mystics were neither good nor evil. But one thing she knew for sure if a man wearing magical symbol and hanging around Satori, it was not by coincidence.

Coupled with Naoma's inability to get a clear read on Darvey when he came in the house and Naoma had more than enough reason to want Darvey out of Satori's life.

Not wanting to let it rest Naoma continued, "Those are very interesting sigils. Don't you think?" Sigil is a word known well in the magic community but not much outside. If Darvey understood the question, Naoma would know he understood much more as well.

"I wouldn't say they are sigils so much," he responded.

Sensing her friendly dinner party was about to be derailed and hoping to stop whatever was happening between them, Satori jumped in, "Did your father ever tell you the meaning or why you should wear it?"

"No. I just always did what he said. He said it would protect me. And so far, it has." He smiled warmly toward Satori and patted her hand.

Naoma thought it was possible his father gave him a talisman to protect his son and this would explain him understanding the word sigil as well. This would also explain why she couldn't sense anything about him. The ring was protecting him. Still, if this was true, his father was a practicing magician. This was too close for comfort for Naoma.

The rest of dinner went along uneventfully even though Naoma never took her eyes off Darvey. Sarah regaled them with stories of her classmates and their dramas. Naoma may not be a fan of Darvey, but Sarah was certainly becoming one.

Darvey insisted on helping clean up the dishes. Satori enjoyed watching him at the sink and wondered if this was what it was like to have a family and a man in the house. Her mother never had a man around and she never lived with anyone either. Sarah and Darvey got in a dish soap bubble battle about halfway through the dishes which put an end to her daydream. Satori broke up the play time before the kitchen turned into a bubbly mess only to end up with bubbles in her hair as well. As much as she wanted to be upset, she thought how wonderful it was to hear laughter and how happy she was Sarah and Darvey got on so easily.

Following the dishes, Sarah went to bed while Satori, Darvey, and Naoma had a cup of coffee and relaxed on the sofas talking. About an hour later, Darvey stood and thanked Satori for a wonderful evening making his way to the coat closet for his jacket.

Both ladies said goodbye and Naoma reassured she was pleased with the encounter. Satori, however, wasn't buying it. Nonetheless, she did appreciate the effort.

Satori waved to Darvey from behind the glass storm door as he drove away and then spun on her heels toward Naoma, "Okay, spill it. What don't you like about him?"

Naoma knew there was no point in playing coy. "Here is the thing, Satori. I told you I sensed something dangerous around you. I still do. I could not get a read on Darvey. Nothing at all. It worries me. I think it is because of the ring he is wearing."

"Christ's sakes Naoma, the only dangerous thing about Darvey is he's stealing my heart. You don't like him because he wears a ring you think blocks you from getting to know him. That's the most ridiculous thing I've heard," Satori snorted. "Trust me, he is a true gentleman, there are no smoke and mirrors with him. Why don't you just get to know him like normal people? Though talking!"

Satori was never going to accept this woo-woo nonsense Naoma always went on about. Thinking she understood what might be the issue, Satori asked the question burning inside her.

"Are you just afraid I will be happy and maybe not need to lean on you so much? Because I will, I will always need you and so will Sarah."

"No dear, I want you to be happy. I know you both will continue to need me and I you. I just can't sense his intentions. I am worried about you and Sarah," she countered.

"Well don't worry about us, we will be fine," Satori insisted.

Naoma took her necklace off. It was one Satori had admired for years. It was beautiful and odd all at the same time. It was a round stone, labradorite, the same kind of stone used to make Satori's heart stone. It was encased in a silver scarab with a moonstone for a back. Its front legs held up a citrine cabochon. It had Egyptian symbols around the outside of the silver encasement.

She handed it to Satori and said, "Fine, I will let it go if you wear this."

Satori didn't know what to say. She was in shock. Partially because she had never touched the necklace before and it was on fire with energy, so much heavier than she expected, and partially because this was Naoma's prized possession. Or so she thought. Satori had never seen her without it. "But, why?" She wondered.

"Because just like the ring protects Darvey this necklace will protect you," Naoma responded, closing her hand around Satori's hands with her necklace inside.

"But what will protect you if you give me your necklace?" Not really understanding why everyone needed so much protection in the middle of a nothing-happens-here town like Wichita. Still it did seem like an obvious question Satori surmised.

Naoma pacified Satori saying she had another one

almost like it at home and Satori placated Naoma promising she would wear it. Naoma made her promise to wear it, even when she sleeps and in the shower. Satori thought Naoma was being a little dramatic; still she agreed with no real intention of following through.

Having felt as though the world was now protected and set right, both ladies went on their way to get ready for bed.

Around eleven Satori was just dozing off, the necklace safely on her nightstand; when her cell buzzed her awake.

It was Darvey.

"Hello," she said hoarsely.

"Satori, are you okay?"

"Why is everyone so freaking worried about my being okay? I am fine, have been fine and will be fine," she snapped back.

Silence...

"I'm Sorry, Darvey, it isn't fair of me. Yes, I am fine. It's just Naoma insisted I start wearing her necklace to protect me. But last I checked only wonderful things have been happening to me, like you for example," she apologized.

"I thought my ring might have been an issue for her. Would it make you feel better if I didn't wear it?" he asked.

"No, please. Wear it. I am not worried about your ring. I am worried because you were here for two hours and didn't try to kiss me once. Worried and a little worked up if I am honest," she purred toward the phone.

He laughed wickedly. "Kitten, it took everything I had not to swallow you whole when I walked in and saw you looking so beautiful in that dress. I think it is my favorite thing you wear."

"You haven't seen all of my outfits yet, Sexy," Satori meowed back to him.

"Challenge accepted, my love," he cajoled.

Satori froze... "My love. My love? Okay calm down," she tried to convince herself as her pulse quickened in her veins. "He didn't say he loved you. It isn't the same thing." she thought to herself.

"Kitten?" he wondered aloud thinking she might have been disconnected.

Satori, suddenly realizing she had been silent longer than would have been required responded, "Yes I am here. I just... never mind. I am here, and I am fine." Regaining her composure she asked why he had called so late. He said it would be better if they could talk in person rather than over the phone. She agreed, saying she didn't have plans in the morning if he wanted to meet for coffee.

"Coffee sounds great!" Darvey agreed.

Knock. Knock. Knock.

A sound came from the front room.

"Are you at my door?" Satori wondered.

"I hope it is okay. I just couldn't sleep. I needed that kiss."

Instantly every atom in Satori's body started vibrating with anticipation.

Satori went to the door to let him in. Almost before the door was even open his arm was around the small of her back pulling her lips to his. The chill from the night air combined with the sensation of his kiss made goose pimples on her skin and her tiny hairs stand straight out. His other hand was on her cheek and in her hair at the same time.

Breathless.

Maybe Satori did need some protection, but it was from herself and the bad decisions she was about to make. Right then she might have wished she kept the necklace on because she was letting this man spend the night even though her daughter was home.

"It's okay." She whispered in Darvey's ear, "As long as you're gone before Sarah wakes up."

She closed the front door with her foot and twisted the lock with her fingers. Then he picked her up and carried Satori back to her room never separating their lips once.

11 The Rear-View Mirror

As the days turned into weeks, the intense relationship Satori and Darvey were creating felt almost magical. Satori was a worrier and just knew something would go wrong, she just was not sure what or when. At the same time, this felt different and incredibly right. They both felt this way. Darvey and Sarah had taken to each other and were practically inseparable. Darvey was becoming part of the family. They spent the weekends together doing family things like going to the zoo, the movies, and the farmers' market.

Naoma had never gotten over her wariness of Darvey; still, she was coming around. There had been zero indications he was anything other than what he shows to Satori. And what he shows is an amazingly generous and loving man who has molded his life to fit Satori's little family. Even though Satori knew Naoma does not trust him, because she cannot see his true nature, there is no awkwardness between them. They laugh and enjoy each other's company at Sunday dinners, which become a new tradition for this modern blended family. The kind of family Satori never knew she always wanted, the family she somehow was always missing. Naoma never knew she wanted either; rather, she needed it. These strong independent women who live next door to each other, and have built their lives alone, together; surprisingly found comfort in when they brought a man in and put him in the mix. A family they never expected.

Naoma had been helping Darvey learn about the symbols on his ring. She believes in allowing a person to learn their own lessons. "Your soul needs to travel its own path," as Naoma always says. Naoma points him in a direction for learning and understanding then allows him to take it from there. So far, Darvey has not seemed very interested, and it was fine with Naoma. To Satori, his disinterest seemed to calm Naoma's fears.

Satori and Naoma hadn't made much progress with Satori's issues, however. They were no closer to figuring out what the danger was around her. Naoma still sensed the danger surrounding Satori and knew she needs to be cautious. As far as finding out who Satori's birth parents are, there haven't been any leads. Satori has a strong suspicion it was someone who was enrolled at Winona in March of 1975 she thinks they should start there and get a list of the students. Satori keeps telling herself she is going to go through the boxes she shipped back from her mom's house. Her mother kept every issue of the Satori publication. Maybe there will be clues. The one in the basket with her when Joyce found her is sitting on top of the rest of the publications inside box number three in her shed.

Satori keeps saying she will get to it next weekend, then next weekend comes, and next weekend goes, and she doesn't go out to the shed. It's hard to say what is stopping her from really researching. A fear of finding out who her parents are? A fear of not being able to find out who they are? Just laziness? Either way, Satori's parents are still hidden in dust and spider webs, under decades of secrets and suspense.

Satori's new family had all started falling in pace with life; the rhythm of it. The loveliness of the daily beats. Not the boring and monotonous part of life but the part that allows you to whittle away twenty years and never accomplish more than mowing your yard and cleaning out your refrigerator each week before you go grocery shopping. It was the beautiful kind of lost that allows you just enough happiness to forget you have goals and plans and dreams beyond today. A satisfaction with now. A spell on your heart and soul which we all long for as much as we dread.

We dread because as soon as we get the peace of presence which allows us to stop fighting for answers and more than what we have, we start accepting the fall. The fall of moving toward the end because if we are not growing we are shrinking. You need only ask the flower to know it is true.

Satori had even stopped driving as hard at work. When she was grieving, she gave one- hundred and fifty percent every day, delivering on timelines before they were even due, and her boss loved her for it. It made him look good, and he benefited from her hard work. Now, in her newfound now-ness she was doing only what she needed, not all she could.

Nathan was starting to give her sideways glances and even worse, he was leveling out the workload between the team. Most people would have appreciated this. Satori did not. To Satori, this was an insult. It was a giant slap in the face. It said you are no longer good enough and I can't trust you will complete all of these tasks. Worse still, come raise and bonus time, you aren't getting what you hoped for. Satori was learning another hard life lesson, don't give too much, even if you have it; because, enough will never again be appreciated.

Driving to work Monday morning Satori was lost in a daydream world of "how can I prove myself worthy again and not give up my life?" when suddenly she was overcome with a gurgling in the pit of her stomach. Her gut lost its gravity joining her throat and her reflexes tightened around the muscles in her neck. Having been pulled firmly back into her reality she knew this wasn't the flu but something more unsettling and far more threatening. She could feel the doom pulling at her. There was a tingling in her back like tentacles tickling at her spine.

Her eyes moved to her rearview mirror instantly. As if looking behind her she would find a squid or jellyfish in the middle of flat lands of Kansas to explain the electrical dance happening in her back. Then she saw a dark navy-blue Chevy, maybe an Impala, defiantly an Impala it was like the police cruisers, following directly behind her.

Suddenly remembering the Impala which followed her around in Winona she thought the coincidence was too much. She remembered what Naoma told her; the car was dangerous. She knew it wasn't Darvey, this whole time, she knew Naoma was wrong, this feeling was completely different from what Darvey made her feel. She was sick to her stomach, she wanted to retch her insides out. She wanted to take a knife and scrape it down her back. Darvey only ever made her feel wonderful and beautiful and lovely. This car was at least two-hundred feet behind her and was making her ill. Whoever was inside it was making her ill.

Looking at it again, she saw there were no other cars on this stretch of 37th Street, which was odd for that time of the morning. Still. Not wanting to do what she normally did, become paranoid and overreact, she tried not to assume anything.

She was only a few blocks from work but needed to test her theory. Rather than turning on Hydraulic for work, she went straight and made a turn on Hillside street instead. The Impala stayed with her. She did several more maneuvers and every time the Chevy was on her tail. She had no doubt she was being followed. Satori's stomach was really churning at this point.

She wondered if she should call the police, but what do you say, there is a car driving in the same direction as me? She already knew their response, "Yes, ma'am. Several I am sure, it is morning traffic, have you missed taking your meds? Is there someone we need to call for you? Do you need to check into a looney bin?" No, thank you! Satori decided the police were not the course of action that would get her where she needed to be right now. Even so, she had watched Law and Order enough to know you need to have proof they are going to harm you or have harmed you to do anything. She can't even see who is in the Impala.

Satori decided the best thing to do was go to work and try to get her work done. So, she headed to work and rather than turning in after her, the Impala continued straight down Hydraulic. Satori got out of her car and went inside the building as quickly as possible. She made several excuses that day to go into Nathan's office. Really, she was just checking the parking lot for a navy blue Impala. The tension left her back a little more each time there were no Impala's, let alone any navy blue cars at all. Satori even started to convince herself she had imagined the entire thing.

By the time Satori left work she had almost forgotten the incident, what still lingered was left as a nagging reprimand for her overactive imagination.

She pulled her 2010 Toyota Prius out of the parking lot and headed home, preoccupying her mind trying to decide between hamburger helper beef stroganoff or shrimp stir-fry for dinner.

She was pulling on to Broadway headed toward the highway when her stomach lurched again. This feeling was getting too familiar and Satori could no longer lie to herself, it was a phantom. She knew this is what danger must feel like, she knew when she looked in her rearview the Impala would be there. She knew it so much she refused to look. She wouldn't give them the satisfaction of her looking for them. She wouldn't connect to them. Not like it mattered, they were there, she knew it, they knew it, She didn't know if they knew she knew, but after the hide and seek this morning, how could they not?

Then Satori remembered how Naoma wanted to know what they looked like and she could not see them this morning. She decided if they were going to follow her, she was going to make sure to get a description of the person driving.

She knew changing lanes didn't help. She slowed down, trying to drop back beside them and the Impala slowed as well and remained behind her. She sped up fast, at least as fast as she was comfortable with, without causing a wreck or getting a ticket, it didn't matter what she tried, there was always something blocking her view, either the sun's reflection, another car, the car visor, something. Satori could not get an unobstructed view and the harder she tried, the more her stomach wanted to hurl all over her car's interior, even though she had skipped lunch and it was empty. She was starting to believe it was an auto-driving car without a driver at all.

Right then her phone rang, it was Naoma.

"Satori, are you okay? Something is wrong." She exclaimed.

"I am fine, Naoma. But the car is following me, the one from Winona, I am sure of it. It is making me very nauseous. It sounds crazy and is a little irritating. What is going on, do you know? Wait, how did you know?" Satori asked her.

"Satori, there are things in this world most people don't understand. They don't try to. Come over when you get home. Are you wearing the necklace I gave you?" Naoma asked.

"Yes."

"Good, but we are going to have to come up with something else," Naoma mumbled. "It doesn't seem to be working anymore. Don't worry about the car; I will take care of it. You just get home," she insisted.

A little relieved to know she wasn't alone, Satori turned her eyes back to the road ahead and determined to get home. No sooner than the phone hung up, two large moving trucks pulled in right behind Satori. The Impala had to slam on its brakes and swerve to avoid a wreck. Satori could have sworn they were not there just a second before, but they had to have been. It wasn't like she was paying attention to anything other than the Impala, anyway. They stayed neck and neck until she was so far ahead she could not even see them anymore. The Impala could not get around them without driving on the shoulder and calling a lot of attention to itself. She pulled off the highway at Zoo Boulevard and went home. No Impala. Naoma had done it.

When Satori got home she went straight to see Naoma, grateful Sarah was with her.

"What is going on," Satori asked as she walked in the door.

"Satori, I am going to tell you something and you just need to believe me, can you do that?" Naoma's face was drawn and tight as she grasped Satori's hands in hers.

"Okay, deal." it was not a deal, Satori had no intention of just blindly believing anything. But more importantly she needed to hear what Naoma had to say. "Will you please tell me?" Satori's mouth widened and her breath left her throat with insistence.

"Have you ever heard of a mystic?" Naoma asked.

"I don't know, you mean like a magician?" Her head was beginning to throb, she didn't understand why Naoma wouldn't just say what she meant.

"Well, kind of, but not like you are thinking. Mystics are real. They can manifest things into reality. Magicians use smoke and mirrors to trick the mind into thinking something has happened when it has not. Mystics have a close spiritual connection to God and the universal spirit. In fact, there are mystics in every religion and mystics who have no religion at all. Just their connection to spirit. I am one of those people, I am a mystic."

"So you're like that kid from those books who goes to that school and gets chosen by a hat, but for religious people?" Satori wondered.

"No. That is a fictional character made up by an author and uses wands and made up practices." Naoma was irritated; Satori was not taking this seriously. "Tell me about something you have lost recently, something you looked everywhere for but couldn't find it." Naoma insisted.

"My favorite pair of glasses, they are blue and red. I haven't seen them in months," she responded.

Naoma closed her eyes for about thirty seconds. You could see her eyeballs moving under her lids. Then she opened them again.

"Look in my cabinet beside the refrigerator." Naoma directed.

"Are you saying I left my glasses there? Why would I have put glasses be in your cabinet, Naoma?" Satori said in disbelief.

"You wouldn't, They wouldn't be there. They would be under your nightstand because you knocked them off in the middle of the night. The fact they are in my cabinet should prove to you I am telling you the truth."

Satori went to her cabinet and opened it. Sitting there, on top of her bag of brown sugar were Satori's blue and red glasses. Instantly, Goosebumps prickled Satori's skin. They must have been obvious because next Naoma told her whenever you have that feeling, it is spirit giving you a sign of confirmation.

"Or it's really cold." Satori retorted. But it wasn't cold and everyone in the room knew it.

"You have my attention, but this doesn't explain why a car is following me and I feel like I am going to throw up," Satori told her.

Naoma explained how she was drawn to this house fifteen years previously. She knew as soon as Satori moved in, she was going to need Naoma's help one day. Satori's aura was strong, powerful, and bright. It has the power to attract people, not always the right people. Naoma is supposed to be Satori's mentor to teach her and train her how to be a mystic. Naoma explained about the long road ahead of Satori. She said since Satori's birthday was on the spring equinox, she had the perfect balance of good and evil and therefore also had a higher propensity to be a successful mystic. Still, it was Satori's choice to learn and become a mystic or to ignore the calling. She also explained regardless if she ignored it or not, others who were mystics, like Naoma would be able to sense Satori's powers and she would always be a target. If she ever hoped to be safe, to be able to keep her daughter safe, Satori would need to at least learn enough to defend herself.

Naoma explained these powers had been dormant and never developed she had been safe so far. Nonetheless, as strong as she was, eventually they had to show up and she was coming into her powers, like it or not. As she matured in life and grew she was going to continue to grow in her strength as well.

Naoma then explained the car following Satori is someone who also knows about her natural abilities and wants to use them for evil. Therefore, it is even more important Satori consider her council.

Satori knew Naoma meant well. She just didn't buy into all the mumbo jumbo. "Naoma, you know I love you. I appreciate all you have done and still do for Sarah and me. But honestly you are freaking me out a little. You are asking me to believe I have some special magical powers because of when I was born, and other people sense this about me. This all somehow puts me in danger. Do you hear how ridiculous this all sounds?" she asked her with sincerity. "You don't, because you really believe it, don't you?.."

Naoma just sighed and stared at Satori. She knew there was nothing you can say to someone who does not believe and refuses to see the truth. You can only meet someone at their level of conciseness and if she isn't ready, you can't beg them into it. She must just continue to be an example and help keep Satori and Sarah safe.

"Naoma, this isn't Hogwarts, and I am not Harry Potter." Satori tried to lighten the mood.

"Forget about Harry fricking Potter, would you!" It was Naoma's turn to start the unraveling.

The two girls had never heard a curse word from Naoma and this was as close as they thought they were ever going to get. They knew she was serious.

"Satori, anyone can be a mystic. With enough work and study and practice, but for you it is a natural gift What I am saying is like it or not, your aura screams the power. People who have to work hard will want to harm you, so they don't have to work so hard, they can just steal it from you," she explained. "I think someone working for the dark side has heard your soul's scream and wants to take it from you. Please let me help you." Naoma couldn't help herself as she made a final plea. She knew she should not be so forceful but she had to try.

"Look I need to process all of this. It just doesn't make sense to me. Sarah and I are going to go home. We can talk more about this tomorrow morning. I will come over before I leave for work," Satori suggested.

Naoma made Satori promise not to make any decisions until they talked more. Satori made her promise to come up with a better way of explaining it. One which seemed based in reality. They both agreed to try, and Satori was going to keep an open mind. She also gave Satori a ring to wear. Naoma said the necklace was not enough protection anymore. What Naoma didn't tell Satori was the ring was more than another talisman for protection. It had an added benefit. While the necklace protects, the ring creates. It helps manifest.

The ring was beautiful. Satori could get on board with the mystic stuff if only for the great jewelry. She had never seen Naoma wear this ring. Naoma explained she had it made for specifically for Satori with stones to bring her strength. There was labradorite, tourmaline, opal, moonstone, amethyst, and black onyx. It was sterling silver and gold. It looked hand forged and old, not newly made. It had a large oval stone on top of dark blue labradorite and five identical stones on either side zigzagging along the side. They were small round stones. A purple amethyst, green tourmaline, blue opal, white moonstone, and black onyx. Surrounding the large stone on top was a bevel made of gold. The wideband tapered down into a small comfortable size with two fan-shaped silver accents and scrollwork. Satori could not take her eyes off it. Satori was truly thankful for her thoughtful gift even if she didn't believe in what Naoma was talking about.

Sarah and Satori went home then Satori called Darvey. She needed to get his take on all this. Maybe he would have some insight. She explained about

Naoma how she was a mystic and she didn't understand anything that was going on around her. He said he would come over and they could talk in person. Satori was so thankful to have him in her life at this moment.

She started making supper and asked Sarah to go do her homework. Huffing in protest Sarah went to her room and got to work. Satori scrapped both of her previous ideas of hamburger helper and stir-fry, tonight was chicken casserole. Throw it in a pan, stick it in the oven and wait till it dings. Satori needed dinner to be mindless tonight. She had enough to think about.

What was all this about? What was she going to do? How could any of this be true? Where did Naoma get such a beautiful ring?

12 Too Close For Comfort

Just as supper was dinging for her attention, Darvey arrived. He didn't even knock anymore, just walked right in. This was fine by everyone in the house. They had fallen into a comfortable pattern. Satori loved how her little house somehow felt even more like a home with this beautiful man so caring and charming and right there, part of it all, part of her life, yes. But also, part of Sarah's.

"Kitten, I'm home," He sang playfully as he walked in.

"Meeooooowwwwwwww" Satori returned.

Indicating not only where to find her but he should come slather her in kisses immediately.

He put his jacket in the closet and took the long way around the living room to the kitchen. "Satori, where did you go?"

Puzzled, she turned to him and said, "I'm right here, silly."

"Oh, I guess I need to get my eyes checked. I didn't see you there." He sauntered over wrapped his arms around her waist and kissed Satori in the middle of her forehead. "Missed you," he whispered against her skin as he kissed it a second time.

She looked up at him with doe eyes, "Me too!" and kissed him on the neck. It drove him crazy to be kissed on his neck and Satori knew it. "Now let me get this on the table before it gets cold," she scooted him away with her hip.

"Where is Sarah?"

"In her room working on her homework, would you mind grabbing her and letting her know supper is ready?"

There was not a room in the house a loud voice couldn't reach, and Sarah's room was literally ten feet away. Nevertheless, Satori learned a long time ago with heartbreak number three or was it number four? Men need to feel useful. She often gave him little tasks even if she could easily have taken care of it herself.

Satori loved these nights where everyone sat around the table talking about their day and plans for the week. It was refreshing to have someone to enjoy it with, other than Sarah of course. It gave her heart a little stop. She liked this little bit of normal she had. Did this have to go away now? Now with what Naoma was trying to get her to believe? Did she have a choice? There were so many questions.

Darvey smiled and mouthed in her direction, "Are you okay?"

Satori half smiled with a grin not quite reaching her eyes and nodded, her head down as she started to clear her plate. Heavy with the growing wonder of what was next.

Finishing dinner and not wanting Sarah to overhear the conversation, Satori gave her the chore of cleaning up after dinner. Clearing the table and doing the dished would keep her busy distracted for a while.

She complained with an adequate amount of pre-teen rambles of unfairness and how wrong human slavery was in a modern world, or any world for that matter, but especially in her own home. Convinced Sarah would survive the ordeal, Satori pulled Darvey into the garage to talk. It was cold in there; so, she was going to make it quick. They could talk more after Sarah went to bed.

Satori began with the account of the Impala, "Something happened today. A car had been following us around in Winona when I was cleaning out Mom's house. That same car was following me today as well," she explained quickly. "I got a weird feeling in my stomach like I wanted to throw up; like I always do when the car gets near. Trust me, I know how weird this sounds. But it gets worse."

"What did the car look like? Did you see who was driving?" Darvey interrupted. Satori was impressed with his chivalry and it made her grin as she began again.

"No. I couldn't get a good look. I just really think there is something dangerous about it and Naoma agrees," she stated.

"Wait; is this something she is putting in your head? You know I really don't like all that magic mumbo-jumbo nonsense she talks about. I don't think it is healthy for Sarah to hear those things." Darvey stated.

Satori was a little choked up at how protective he was being with Sarah. She had almost given up on finding a father figure for her and Darvey had been sounding more and more like one every day.

"Darvey, I am serious," Satori reassured, "Naoma was telling me tonight she wants to teach me how to start taking care of myself."

"Look, we can talk more after Sarah is in bed, but that is basically what... Ahhhh"

She grabbed at her stomach and bucked over with a wave of bile that nearly reached her throat Satori choked out. "I'm going to be sick."

"Something is wrong."

Looking in front of the house, she could see the Impala. "The car is here, it is close!"

Then she looked over and saw three men entering through the front door. "Damn this safe trusting neighborhood and always leaving the front door open with the just the screen door shut and never locked," Satori thought.

At that very moment, she got a strong pull it felt almost like someone had tied a rope to her hips and the ground and was tugging backward against it hard, she knew she could not to leave the garage. "Sarah is in trouble Darvey, please go help her," Satori stammered.

Darvey turned quickly going back in the house. Satori could hear voices and yelling but she couldn't tell what they were saying. The nausea was so strong at this point, she was practically doubled over wishing the vomit would just come out so the feeling would pass, and she could go help her family.

Just then the garage door opened, and a bright light from the dining room chandelier poured on to Satori's face. She hadn't realized she and Darvey had been talking in the garage with just the light from the garage door windows peaking in. One of the men was looking in the garage for something, and she knew without them saying anything it was her. He looked directly at her, but he couldn't see her. She was right in front of him. Why couldn't he see her? Why were they looking for her? Satori wondered. She doesn't have any of these powers Naoma told her about. So why do they want her? She can't help them. Again, she felt the tug pulling her further into in the garage.

Then she heard Sarah scream. "No! Mom! Help!"

Not Sarah god damn it! Satori instantly broke the invisible bonds holding her. She followed the man back into the house through the garage door before it closed behind him. Somehow, she knew none of the men could see her even if she didn't understand why or how.

Sarah was being held down on the sofa. One of the men was sitting on the sofa and had his arms around her from behind clasped tight around her. She was kicking and flailing but it was no use. Darvey was on the ground, unconscious. Satori assumed one of the men must have knocked him out.

The man who had just been in the garage was in front of Sarah. He said to her in a sickening voice which sounded both gruff and sleazy, "We know you are here, little momma. We can feel you. You better come out before we make your daughter pay your price. It's all the same to us."

Satori was stunned. In shock. What the hell was going on here? Why couldn't they see her? she wondered. What did they want from her?

The man spoke again, "Your mom wants to play hide and seek with us. Guess you'll have to do instead."

Satori's blood boiled. Beneath her shirt, she could feel her chest exploding with the thumping of adrenaline and rage. Her heart was racing with terror and determination.

She reached out, but as she did she realized her arms weren't actually moving. She was visualizing it. She saw her hand grasping for the men's hearts, all three of the men's hearts at the same time. She looked at their pulsing hearts in her hand as they merged into one beating monstrosity. Her breath quickened and deepened as she realized she was holding their lives in her hands and not the other way around. The power was as intoxicating as it was terrifying.

She began to squeeze the organ in her hand and looked up at the men. One standing watch over her motionless lover, one restraining her beautiful child, and one barely feet in front of her threatening the life of her daughter if she didn't show herself.

Simultaneously, all three buckled and collapsed clutching their chests.

Never opening her mouth Satori screamed at them in her mind, "Get out you bastards."

Finally gaining some footing herself now she was in control, Satori began speaking out loud. "Who the hell do you think you are to come in my home and threaten me and my family?"

Suddenly all three men turned to look directly at her. Everyone could see her now, even Sarah. Running to her mother she grabbed her waist and hid behind her, squatting on the floor.

Satori focused on their eyes all three at the same time and said in her mind again, "Now." She gave one final squeeze in with her minds eyes of the heart she was holding and then released the grip. She still held on to their hearts. She joined her palms together with her fingers splayed and fanning outward. She pulled her hand to her own heart and then pushed out against the air in the room willing the men to leave and take every bit of their invasion with them.

She banished them, "You are not welcome in my home!"

The men all scooted with her gesture an equal distance on the floor, the exception being the man who had been on the sofa holding Sarah who rolled off onto the floor.

Instantly, they were scrambling like dogs on a wet tile floor. The three men jockeyed for footing and ran to the door crawling over each other. Their eyes were the size of silver dollars and their mouths were tight lines not betraying a word to each other as they clawed their way out.

Satori ran after them as far as the front door and was beginning to lock it when she saw Naoma coming around the corner onto the porch. Satori hurried her inside and locked the door, realizing the safety she had known and loved in this cozy little street was now bitterly destroyed.

"Are you okay?" Naoma spurted. "Is Sarah?"

Satori was nodding her head slowly. Still trying to make sense of everything that just happened.

Naoma, was at Sarah's side checking her over for bruises, breaks or blood. She found none. Sarah had buried her head in Naoma's lap and was sobbing. Naoma was comforting her with soft gentle pats to her back and arm.

Satori was still leaning on the door like an opossum playing dead. Naoma looked at her. "What were you thinking Satori? You could have been killed. I told you to stay put."

Satori turned her attention to Naoma. "You made me stay in the garage? How is that even possible?

They were going to hurt Sarah! Do you think I care if anything happens to me if they were going to hurt her."

With her faculties returning, Satori ran to Sarah to see if she was okay. Sarah was shaking and crying but physically, she appeared to be fine. Bruises were appearing on her arms where she had been restrained by those monsters.

"Bastards," Satori mumbled under her breath.

Suddenly she remembered Darvey was unconscious on the floor. "Stay with her," she told Naoma.

Satori went to Darvey who was starting to come around. "Darvey... Darvey... Are you okay? Can you hear me? Where did they hit you? I am going to get frozen peas."

He was still groggy, but he was going to be okay. Satori reached to help him balance himself as he sat up and he took her hand. They nearly toppled over together when he tried leveraging against her to get up. She had better intentions than strength.

"Sarah, is she okay?" he asked.

"Yes, she is fine, shaken up, bruised, but fine. What happened? What did you see?"

"The last thing I remember is coming in and seeing them dragging Sarah, next thing I know there was a thump to the side of my face then you waking me up. It hurts like a mother."

"Let me go get you those peas. Sarah, do you need ice sweetheart?" Satori questioned and kissed her forehead as she passed her into the kitchen.

Satori noticed the dinner mess still needed cleaning and now there was an even bigger mess as it appeared Sarah was taking the left over casserole to the counter when they grabbed her. It was now all over the floor and the glass dish was in shards across the navy-blue tile.

"That was a lot of trouble just to get out of doing the dishes, Sarah." Satori teased.

Silence.

"Too soon…" Satori followed up and achieved the result she was seeking when Sarah giggled.

Satori was relieved. While she knew what just transpired would have a heavy toll on her baby girl for many years, the fact she should could still get a giggle out of her was a sign all was not lost.

She returned in with the peas for Darvey and green beans for Sarah. Sarah didn't say she needed them, but Satori brought them anyway.

The quartet sat there for a while, just trying to make sense of everything in their own minds. Each of them dazed and uncertain how to approach the topic.

They didn't see me, Satori thought. How is it possible?

Naoma spoke as if she's read Satori's thoughts. "They couldn't see you because of the ring."

"Satori dear, you know we have a connection. I can hear your thoughts when you need me to and you know out of everyone in this room, the one person you want to ask is me. Which is why I heard you ask."

"Mom, Naoma can read your mind? Ummm… Freaky!!" Sarah said. "Will you show me how, Naoma?"

Satori shook her head, "Sarah, we aren't going to talk about this right now."

"Can I sleep with you tonight? Sarah asked.

"Try not to."

Sarah responded by throwing her arms around her

mother. "I love you, Mommy."

"I love you too, sweetheart," Satori replied, and softly kissed her on her beautiful intact head.

Sarah went to get her pajamas on while Naoma helped Satori clean the mess in the kitchen. Darvey declared he was staying the night and asked where Satori kept a spare blanket and pillow for the sofa. She tried telling him it wasn't necessary, but honestly, she was grateful he was staying. Satori was terrified the men might come back.

For a minute Satori thought Naoma was even going to insist on sleeping on the loveseat. They decided Satori would take the next day off work for a family emergency. If this didn't qualify, what did? Naoma sighed in relief and asked Satori to come over as soon as they were up. There was a lot to talk about. Satori agreed and Darvey walked Naoma home. It was just next door, but after his miserable performance trying to save the day with Sarah, Darvey needed to redeem himself.

By the time he returned Sarah was already asleep in bed and Satori was in her pajama's. They were her cozy knit jammies. Soft and snuggly. So, when she went to give Darvey a hug and kiss goodnight he just wanted to rub all over her. Which made her want to rub all over him. Rubbing all over each other and life threatening drama kind of go hand in hand. Daughters' in beds, however, do not.

They both stopped, understanding now was not the time to let their guard down.

Darvey's deep brown eyes stared deep into Satori's. Their arms were tight around each other. There was a smile on his face as if he had a secret he wasn't going to tell.

Returning his smile she asked, "What's that look about?" He just shook his head. "You better spill it mister, my hands are awfully close to your arm pits and we both know what happens when I get too close to them. You start squirming like a little girl."

"It's just you are so beautiful, Satori. Sometimes I wonder how I ever my lived my life without you. What did I do? What did I think about? What mattered to me? I can't even remember anything before you." He sighed deeply then leaned down and kissed her softly on the lips, caressing her lower lip with his tongue and then giving a soft bite. "You take my breath away. You are so strong and such a fighter. You don't need me in your life, but you've welcomed me in and allowed me to be part of your daughter's life as well. I'm just so overwhelmed with emotion. Satori, if anything had happened to either of you tonight, I would be lost."

Satori's eyes started welling up with tears. He moved his hands up to her face and pulled his thumbs under each of her eyes catching and drying the tears.

"Satori, I think I... No, I know I have fallen in love with you. Deeply. Madly. Completely in love with you. I don't want to spend another day of my life without you in it one-hundred percent. Please don't say anything. Just think about what you feel and what ------ - might mean in your life. When we figure this all out we can talk more."

"Oh Darvey," she started.

He closed her mouth with his lips. And whispered, "Sshhh," softly onto them. "You need to sleep. I'll be here when you wake up, my love."

They kissed goodnight with a deep meaningful kiss saying everything clearly without words. She went to her room. She knew she loved Darvey but she also knew he gave her a gift in that moment, one where she can think about what saying those words means and how it changes not only her life but the life of her daughter. And to know if she is truly ready for everything it implies even if she knows she does love him, truly, as well.

Darvey turned out the lights, got down to his boxer briefs and settled into the sofa.

Satori had two thoughts as she fell asleep. One: What the hell is going on here? and two: He loves me, this god of a man really loves me!

13 No Boys Allowed

Considering everything that happened the day before, Satori couldn't believe she slept. The kicks and punches from Sarah didn't even bother her enough to wake her. She knew one day she would miss the nighttime jujitsu matches of her baby girl, but today was not that day. She was still firmly wishing for a decent night's sleep when she let her daughter stay in her room and was thankful she'd had one. She was equally surprised it came after such an eventful evening. Both with her mentally squeezing the hearts of intruders and with Darvey squeezing hers. Darvey. He loved her! The thought brightened her mood instantly.

In fact, what woke Satori, since she turned off her alarm after texting Nathan to tell him she was taking the day off, was the smell of bacon. She was a little better than a begging dog when it came to bacon and Darvey knew it. He did not have to go to all this trouble to get an "I love you" back, but hey. Satori

141

figured she would soak it up while it lasted.

She looked at Sarah who was sprawled almost sideways on the bed, her hair covering half her face and drool in a puddle on the pillow just below her mouth. Satori was half in love with her little sleeping angel and half disgusted by the puddle of drool. She scrunched up her face a little and remembered; she is growing up. So, she just took a minute to enjoy watching her sleeping face a little longer. Besides, it would be a day full of wall bouncing in no time as soon as the bacon found its way to her nostrils. Sarah took after her mom in this way.

Satori got out of bed, headed to the bathroom and let go of an entire night's worth of kidney juice. When she was finished, she found her way the few feet down the hall to the side entrance into the kitchen. Darvey was standing there in just his jeans and Satori's frilliest apron. Satori could barely contain her laughter. He was as adorable as he was ridiculous and she wanted to rub her hands all over his beautiful pecks. Then she noticed Darvey had been there a while because he had completely cleaned the kitchen. So well in fact he felt safe walking on the floor in his bare feet. Even though he had an apron on, it did nothing to hide his chiseled chest. Every time he moved the bacon around in the pan the muscles in his arms flexed and reminded Satori how strong and sexy he truly was. His hair was adorably tousled, having not bothered to straighten it since he woke up. She didn't think he had even run his fingers through it. Satori was really wishing they were alone in the house right then.

"Good morning, Sexy," she smiled. "Sleep well?"

"I think you have the most comfortable sofa I have

ever slept on," he responded. "And good morning to you too, Kitten." He leaned over to her with a quick kiss.

"What ch'a making?" Satori asked.

"It's a surprise. But I will tell you it includes bacon, eggs, and bread. And I have been told eating this is an experience unlike any other in the world. Strike that, the Universe. It. Is. That. Good," he boasted. And gave one of his beautiful half-cocked smiles Satori couldn't help but swoon over.

"Oh really. So you have made this for a lot of women I take it."

"No, just my niece. She loves it. Mind you she hasn't experienced everything in the universe, but I have never known her to lie."

"So how long until we get to enjoy your treat?" Satori asked.

"About another ten minutes," Darvey leaned over to give her another kiss before spanking her bottom with the spatula.

"Okay, well you go put your shirt on Mr. Sexy Pants, and I will watch the bacon. Sarah has no need of seeing this spectacle in our kitchen. You sir are rated R for sure."

Darvey smiled and handed her the spatula. As he was walking out of the kitchen he took the apron off placing it on her shoulder, "One last look before the show is over Ms. Stone." Darvey backed out of the kitchen finding his way back to the living room.

Darvey finished his prized egg sandwiches and called the girls to the table. They were truly amazing. Both Satori and Sarah devoured the buttery deliciousness as soon as they took their first bite. They hoped this was going to start to be a regular occurrence in the Stone-Lavender household.

After breakfast, Satori explained to Darvey she needed to go talk with Naoma alone. By alone she only meant sans Darvey but didn't know how else to tell him. Naoma wanted to explain what she was talking about and what happened last night. He understood and said if she needed anything just to let him know and he would be there. Satori truly appreciated how understanding he was about everything. It seemed things were perfect. The scary kind of perfect. The wrench is coming kind of perfect. But she was trying not to think of the wrench right now. No wrenches, not now. There was too much going on and she really needed Darvey to be good, to stay perfect. She wasn't going to allow herself to toss the Texas sized wrench in the middle of this perfect man and their relationship.

Satori waited for Sarah to get dressed and then they went over to Naoma's house.

Naoma wasted no time. "First things first," she said. "Your friend with the daughter Sarah's age. Do you think she would let Sarah stay with her for a few days?"

"Nicole? I am sure she would. But, I am not letting Sarah out of my sight, are you insane? Someone tried to hurt her less than twelve hours ago." Satori insisted.

"Sarah you need to trust me. I can protect her, I had this made. My friend makes these Quantum Stones and infuses them with frequencies. Then when I get them I do a little something to them myself. It will keep her from being seen by anyone who would want to harm her. It works just like the one I gave you." Naoma explained.

It was a necklace; similar to the one she had originally given Satori. Only this one was a clear blue flash labradorite donut shaped flat stone, with a silver swirl wire spiraling into the center where a purple amethyst triangular cut gem sat.

"Mine stopped working, how do you know hers won't stop as well?" Satori asked.

"Yours hasn't stopped working, the men in the house, they couldn't see you remember. Not until you spoke out loud directly to them." Naoma reminded her.

"Yes but the car is following me..." Satori retorted. "And you said yourself it wasn't working anymore, and you needed to strengthen it,"

"That car was following your car, not you. Remember how you couldn't see the driver, yes? Well, it's because they had a charm just like you. From now on you will drive my car. They have figured out what you drive. And the ring did strengthen your natural energies..."

Satori wasn't sure what she was talking about. What natural energies? She started thinking about the events of the night before, "Oh, when I grabbed their hearts?" she asked.

"No, before then. When you got sick to your stomach, it was worse than before wasn't it?" Naoma asked.

"Yes."

"And then when you saw their car and the men coming in the front door... do you remember?"

"Yes, I do but how is that different than normal, I see normally."

"Do you normally see through brick walls."

Thinking again for a moment Satori remembered,

the only light in the garage came through once the dining room door opened.

"The garage door was down and the house door was shut. I couldn't have seen them or their car. Then how did I?"

"Because you needed to and you willed yourself to know the answer. So you saw what you needed to see. You energy expanded. You used your third eye." Naoma explain.

"So you are saying I can see things, anything I want. If I wear this ring, like it is magic or something." Satori asked.

"No, it isn't magic. It's spirit, energy if you will. It is getting in touch with your higher self. With the goddess inside of you. You need the ring now, but if you learn the way, if you follow the truth, you will be able to elevate your energy when you need to and manifest anything you imagine. And with practice and trust in the universal spirit, some refer to as, God, you can even manifest things almost immediately," she explained. "This Satori is the last piece of my personal dharma in this lifetime. To teach you the ways of the mystic."

"Your last dharma? Don't you mean karma?" Satori asked

"No, dharma. It basically signifies what I have been called to do. The work put before me to continue God's work on earth. I have studied my entire life, spending time learning the lessons. It is not a quick or easy process. It won't be for your either. Don't worry, my time is not near."

"So I guess that means I really don't have much of a choice then. Either I learn from you, or some "thing" or some "one" out there will kill me or my loved ones trying to get this – whatever it is – from me." Satori reasoned.

"Everything is a choice, Satori. Every choice has a consequence, sometimes we interpret it as good and sometimes we interpret it as bad. Not making a choice has a consequence too. But you absolutely have a choice. You must make the choice because if you begin this study with impure motives it will not be fruitful. You get back equal measure to what you put in," Naoma explained.

"I think I understand." Satori said, "Let me go call Nicole and get Sarah packed up. How long do you think she will need to be away?"

"Only a couple days. I believe the reason they are trying right now is because your birthday is coming up. Wednesday, right? It is when your connection to spirit is strongest. And like I said earlier, your birth was on the spring equinox. The Equinox carries its own power which amplifies what you have naturally. I think they are planning to take your energy from you on your birthday. If she can stay with her until then, I believe she will be safe."

Then Naoma became quiet, "Satori, please don't say anything to Darvey just yet. We don't know how they are getting their information. They can pull it from him without him even knowing. You will jeopardize Sarah and your friends' safety if you tell what we are doing. Where she is staying."

Satori found herself up against a road block she couldn't handle now. There was no way Darvey would let anyone know something that could hurt her and Sarah. She knew this without a doubt. Still, how could she take any chances with Sarah's life? What if it was against Darvey's will, or something Darvey didn't even know was happening? For now, Satori would not say anything to him. She may not understand but she did know Sarah's safety was the single most important thing, above her own, above all else.

"I understand."

But the only thing Satori truly understood was how scared she was, how much she wanted to protect her daughter, and how much she wished she could go back to those care free days – before – Christmas when her mother told her she had Cancer and her life was thrown the biggest wrench she'd ever known. Although, she thought, she would keep Darvey, if it was all the same. ⬚

14 Saying Goodbye

It was difficult trying to explain to Sarah, why, after everything that just happened, she had to stay at Nicole's for a few days. Luckily it was spring break at school so she wasn't going to be missing out on any school work. Sarah didn't think that part was so lucky. Still, with both her and Alexis out of school they would be excited to spend time together.

Sarah was still shaken up over the night before. So, when Naoma came over and gave her the necklace she had prepared for her, Sarah brightened. Naoma explained it was critically important the necklace not come off. Not even in the shower or at night. She said as long as she wore the necklace, no one who intended to harm her could see her. She also explained how it would also work if she didn't intend to be seen. Like when playing hide and seek. However, once she was she was seen the effect was over.

Sarah thought this was all pretty cool, the power

of invisibility. She thought this would come in handy during class when she didn't want to read out loud or answer questions.

The girls packed Naoma's car with Sarah's suitcase and drove ten miles to the other side of town where Nicole lived. Sarah and Satori often held hands when driving in the car. This time though. They were hanging on for dear life, their palms were sweating as they hung on to each other. Both so scared to let go, knowing soon they would have to. Satori was trying hard to trust Naoma and trying not to let Sarah see how little faith she truly had.

The only person she had ever truly been able to count on was herself, and the second person she counted on, her mother, had died last March. Satori felt alone, scared, and she had no idea how to get her and Sarah through this. She had no faith in trinkets of jewelry. She was terrified to let her daughter, the only thing that truly mattered to her, out of her sight. And that was exactly what she was about to do. No matter what she was getting to face, how could she face it with part of her soul half way across town worrying about her baby girl.

Satori could sense Sarah had some of the same thoughts or at least some of the fear.

Finally, Sarah piped up with, "Mom, who is going to take care of you while I am gone? I might be safe, but who is keeping you safe?"

"Oh, love bug, you don't need to worry about me. I'm strong, I am a fighter, and I will be fine. You saw how I took care of those goons who wanted to hurt you. What makes you think I need a protector?" Satori wasn't sure if I was trying to convince Sarah or herself.

She had no idea how she was able to do what she did, for all she knew it was Naoma who did it. Satori was terrified. She was scared of the people who seemingly wanted to use her for some dark purpose and she was scared of what Naoma was going to teach her. She was terrified of Darvey saying he loved her. Everything had been good, perfect even. Why did it need to change now?

Satori cared for Darvey, deeply. He had become her rock, and she enjoyed having him around. But love was another level. It meant we would have to change our lives and become different people. She wasn't sure she was ready to give up her freedom or independence. She knew she loved him, or at least she lusted him, that was without question. She enjoyed him. But, love? Maybe.

When they arrived at Nicole's, she and Alexis were on the porch waiting. The girls in unison pointed and said there she is. Nicole and Satori smiled at each other with a grin indicating how happy we were the girls liked each other so much. There really wasn't a reason not to, they had been around each other from birth. They pulled in the drive way and Sarah flung herself from the car and ran to Alexis. The girls were squealing, "I can't believe you get to stay with us for spring break!" Alexis exclaimed.

"I know right!!"

Satori went to the back of the car to collect Sarah's suitcase and carried it Nicole's front door.

"Are you going to tell me what's going on?" Nicole asked.

"I wouldn't know where to start."

The women walked in and Satori told Sarah to take her bag to Alexis's room. The girls flew off to the basement.

"So, spill it." Nicole insisted.

"Darvey told me he loved me?!" Satori said with a question hoping it would pacify Nicole needing a better reason.

"Oh. My. god. Are you serious? That's a pretty big step. Satori I swear, I have no idea how you landed such a hunk of a man. And so kind and generous. I mean not that you aren't a knock out yourself. You are, Girl, you know you are! But what are the odds you would be sitting on the same flight twice. And the whole thing about your "eyes" he has always been looking for or something. I mean you have to admit this is all a little crazy."

"So, is that why she needs to stay with me. You and Darvey need some alone time?" Nicole somehow managed to combine air quotes, an elbow in the side, and a hip gyration all at the same time.

"No," Satori giggled. "Although it'd be a heck of a'lot better than reality. Will you do me a favor and start writing my life story? All I can seem to do is mess it up."

The women laughed as coffee was poured. Nicole always made the best coffee. She goes to a store in downtown Wichita called the Spice Merchant. They roast their own beans right in the store. It always smells amazing in there. Satori, on the other hand, just gets whatever brand is cheapest on the shelf at Dillon's. Satori's coffee is not amazing. Having coffee at Nicole's house is an experience, and she never turns down a cup. Today she brewed Balinese Blue Moon. It is so rich and delicious. The coffee almost makes Satori want to start grinding her own beans. Almost.

"So, then what was so important you had to rush over with Sarah. Are you okay or sick or something? And why are you driving a little ford SUV. Is it Darvey's car, it doesn't look like him…" she trailed off peeking out the window.

"It's Naoma's car," Satori explained. "This is going to sound unbelievable, I know. Just bear with me, Okay?"

She nodded.

"So, Naoma thinks I am in danger. And I guess I do too. I mean, Sarah might talk about it so I should tell you what happened. Someone - three someone's actually came to the house last night trying to find me. The just walked right in the front door. Darvey and I were in the garage but Sarah was in the kitchen cleaning up after dinner. They grabbed her and Darvey went in to be the hero, only rather than the hero they knocked him out cold on the floor."

Nicole covered her mouth and gasped. "Oh my goodness, Satori. What happened? I mean, how are you both…? What…?"

Satori continued, "I heard Sarah screaming and ran in the house, I guess I scared them off or something because they went running from the house," she finished, knowing this version was the best one to tell her friend. All the weird hocus-pocus wasn't going to go over well and might end with a call to the looney bin.

"Wow. I mean. Wow. What the Hell?" Nicole pondered. "What did the police say about it all? Do they think you are in danger?"

Satori was dumbfounded. "I didn't even think to call the police. It makes a lot of sense…" she shook her head in disgust at her ignorance. "Do you think it is too late to call at this point?"

"No. Why didn't you call them last night? That would have been the first thing I did. Right after I changed my pants." Nicole stated.

"Well, Naoma showed up right after they left. You know how I have always said she is a little weird or off somehow? Well, she started telling me why. It is all weird and hokey and I don't know if I believe her completely but she thinks she can help me. She gave Sarah a necklace and said it will keep her safe. She also said not to tell anyone where Sarah is. So don't let the girls post on Facebook or anything social please. She thinks everything will be fine after my birthday," Satori loved and trusted Nicole, but she wasn't comfortable sharing any more.

Nicole nodded her head in agreement, "Yes of course. You are stronger than I am. I could never let my kids out of my site if they were in danger. I hate asking this, but are we safe, I mean with her here."

"Yes, of course, they are after me, not her. If no one knows she is here, then you are all safe. And she is safer not being around me right now." Satori assured herself and Nicole.

"Satori, sweetie. How are you holding up to all this? I would be a basket case. I almost am and it isn't even happening to me," said Nicole.

"I am doing fine. I mean considering... Darvey stayed over and slept on the sofa. It helped me sleep easier. You should have seen him this morning. He put on my old fifties apron, the one with the flowers and ruffles. Then he cooked us breakfast. He was ridiculously cute and sexy. I kind of wished Sarah hadn't been there this morning." Satori confessed with a mischievous grin.

"Careful Satori or you will end up with a house full like I have. Speaking of which, it's way too quiet. Alexis. Sarah," she hollered to the girls in the basement. And the girls giggled in return confirming they were just fine.

"Okay, so Sarah is safe here and we are safe with her here as long as we don't tell anyone. But what about you? How dangerous is this? I mean, is this the last time I will see you?." Nicole asked. Everything started to hit home very fast for Satori. She hadn't really thought about it that way before. How dangerous was it? She didn't have time to think about it now either.

Reaching over to give her friend a hug she tried to reassure her.

"No," Satori affirmed. "I will be damned if anyone or anything will take me from Sarah or you or everyone else I love. Don't even think that way."

"Okay, so you will be here by this weekend to get her, Right Satori!?"

Satori nodded her head in agreement.

"This is a lot Satori. How am I supposed to not worry?" Nicole wondered. Her friend was trusting her with her daughter and she truly didn't know how much danger she was really in. Nicole was terrified but didn't want to let Satori or Sarah know.

"I don't know. I can't tell you how not to worry Nicole. I just know in my heart, it is going to be okay. You must believe me I just have this gut feeling everything is going to be okay and I know if you are taking care of Sarah, I can focus. I love you for doing this. Oh, hell. I just love you!" Satori reassured her.

But she didn't know. Satori's stomach was in knots but not because some danger was near, it was because she was scared to death. But more than anything she needed Nicole to believe everything would be okay. She needed Nicole to be safe and secure so she could keep Sarah the same way.

Sarah and Alexis came upstairs. "Hey do you think we can go to the mall one day this week?" they both asked.

"Not alone," the women said in unison and broke out in laughter.

The girls just looked at each other like their moms had lost their minds. They were used to the Satori/Nicole show by now, they always joked they should have their own reality show. It was non-stop laughter when those two were together.

"Come give me a hug love bug. I need to get going." Satori said to Sarah.

Sarah ran over and hugged her mom tight, so tight Satori thought she might never let go.

Satori moved the hair out of her face and gently caressed the bridge of her nose. Ever since she was a baby, this was the way her mother soothed her. She used to fall asleep in about thirty seconds this way.

"I'll see you this weekend," Satori whispered to the top of her head. "You are going to have so much fun with Alexis and Nicole. The weekend will be here before you know it."

"I'm going to miss your birthday Mom."

Satori's throat caught. She had not thought of that. Birthdays were always special between them. They spent the day together. Well with the exception of Sarah's last one which Satori forgot.

"I know. We will celebrate this weekend. Deal?"

Sarah nodded her agreement.

"Okay, now be strong and know I love you more

than anything! You are my heart walking outside my body. You are the best thing I have ever done. I am going to be fine. Wear your necklace, don't take it off no matter what, promise me! Brush your teeth and mind Nicole. Okay?" Satori spoke and fought the tears from her eyes not wanting Sarah to see how scared she really was.

Sarah hugged her mom tighter.

"You didn't say I had to shower. So does it mean I don't have to?"

"No. You absolutely must shower. You don't want to stink Nicole's family out of their house do you?"

They giggled, both from the thought and from the severity of what they knew they had been through and were going through.

"I love you buggy," she said finally.

Sarah let go and walked her mom to the door.

"I'll see you this weekend," she smiled at her daughter one last time not sure if the smile was for herself, her daughter, or her best friend.

Satori turned and walked to the car. Tears welling up in her eyes. She couldn't let Sarah see her like this. Scared. Unsure. Weak.

She got to the car and waved goodbye as she pulled out. Satori could see her in the rearview mirror watching her all the way down the road until she turned out of the cul-de-sac.

Stopping at the sign right at the edge of Nicole's community, Satori closed her eyes and said a prayer.

15 Lesson #1

Satori got back to Naoma's around noon pulling the car into Naoma's garage. Satori went in to find her waiting inside on the sofa with a cup of tea. "Are you hungry," Naoma asked.

Still full from the breakfast Darvey fixed Satori just shook her head. With a deep sigh Satori joined her new teacher on the sofa.

"So, where do we start? How are we going to save my life?" she asked.

Naoma began, "Well, I think we should start with a general understanding of what spirituality is."

"I went to Sunday school, I know what spirituality is," Satori responded. She was a little offended. There wasn't a lot of time and she didn't want to waste it on such elementary things.

"The church you were part of wasn't spirituality, not true spirituality. It was religion. If it had been, you would likely still be there. Because once you truly feel spirits gift in your life, you don't turn away. Religion, good or bad, is always someone else's interpretation of what spirituality was intended to be. It all starts with good intent, then to help make spirituality digestible and understandable for everyone along the way it gets changed. Men often have good intent but sometimes it gets lost along the way."

Naoma went on to explain the problem is after thousands of years and countless leaders and all the human egos have been involved, spirituality has been lost inside many of the world's religions. True spirituality is felt, in your heart. It can be pointed to, one can be guided, but no definitive source can be found, it isn't something you can find in Sunday school or outside of the individual person. You can't define it. We must each "know" spiritually for ourselves. Religions can help some people to find their way but they can also hinder some people.

Naoma asked if Satori remembered in Sunday school if any of the other kids were given special treatment for being better behaved or reading more lessons. Satori told her they had, just as in regular school. She then asked about the adults. Did any of them ever look at her with disdain or judgment? She said they had. This is in fact what had lead Satori away from the church in the first place. She still loved and believed in God, but she didn't feel at home when she was at church. She never felt good enough to be there.

Naoma explained over the next couple of hours this is because many religions are not teaching people to find God for themselves. They are teaching their flocks there is only one way into heaven and all other ways are wrong. The put fear in the hearts teaching if they stray from their message they will be cast out from heaven and not accepted by God. But it wasn't the truth. She also said Satori should not trust anyone, not even her. She should only trust what feels true in her own heart. She can learn and gain wisdom from many sources but trust most what is in her own heart. And listen closest to the silence and stillness of her mind in meditation or prayer. Because what she is really listening to is the energy of the universe, the one spirit connects us all. Some call this Universe, Spirit or God. God doesn't care what we call him. It is only important that we know him, that we feel the spirit in each of us and that we understand we are all one.

To help Satori understand this better, she told her to think of a conversation she had with someone recently, any conversation. Naoma asked Satori to replay it in her head.

Satori thought about the conversation she had with Darvey that morning. When she was finished, she said, "So you just had a thought. Did you hear the words as you were thinking it?"

"Yes."

"Did you hear the words with your ears?"

"Well no…"

"So how did you hear them? Who is it that was observing the thought in your head?"

"You were having the thought."

"You mind was busy with the thinking of it. So who, was hearing it? Who was watching it on the movie reel in your mind? You didn't see it with your actual eyes. There is something else inside of you. The something is inside all of us. It is the observer and we are the observed. We are a single expression of divinity."

"When we are mindful, we can observe the observer. We can observe Spirit within each of us."

Satori was confused and Naoma could see it on her face. She was going to have to try explaining it another way.

"Satori, You are a single point of creation which the universe or God has chosen to manifest into this world. You are here to learn lessons and grow spiritually. We all are, everything in all of existence is part of everything else. We all come from the same source and we will all one day return to source. It doesn't matter what you believe or don't believe, it is a truth. The first step in learning the ways of the mystic is to understand this concept. To discover the I AM-ness of yourself. You must learn to understand you alone create your own Heaven or Hell on earth. The universe responds to whatever you think, but more importantly, what you feel. Thoughts are vibrations, feelings are vibrations, and actions are vibrations." Naoma explained.

She continued, "Remember when the bible said, "That which you do to the least of my brethren, you do unto me." This was a pointer to the truth. The truth that we are all connected. When you hate someone, you hate yourself; because they are part of you and you them. When you love someone, you love part of yourself. This is also why it is said if you lack something give it away. You are giving it to yourself."

Naoma continued, "You say all the time you just mess everything up in your life. Then you wait around until it happens and say, 'see I told you so.' What you need to try is to change the message. You could say, I used to create negativity in my life because I did not know I had a choice. Now I know I have a choice and I choose positive outcomes. When you see someone in trouble, help them. When you are presented with an opportunity to help, do so. You create vibrations so problems are solved. If you leave them without helping, you create vibrations where we are on our own for problems." Naoma paused to check for understanding.

Satori still looked dazed, but it was beginning to make sense as well.

"The thing you must understand Satori, is most of us don't realize what we have done until the flat tire has us on the side of the road. The key is realization," she continued.

"You must first realize what you are doing to sabotage your life and then you can begin to change the thought patterns."

Naoma explained how the true destination of spirit was higher vibrational frequencies. She said Spirit is neutral. Spirit wants what will bring the highest vibrational change for good. She asked Satori to think of a religious war. Both sides think they are fighting for the greatest good. They believe if they win, they will be doing God's work. They are both right. But they are fighting for same thing. You see, when the battle is forged the winning side is the one that will be most joyous, most happy, with the greatest number of people being served and feeling blessed. Even if it means for that to happen the same number of people minus one would feel defeated. Because there usually are winners and losers.

"It is called the 'Half plus One Rule,'" Naoma explained.

Because the net sum would create a positive outcome, the victor would be the half plus one group.

Because positive vibrations are at a higher frequency than lower vibrations. Happiness trumps sadness, this is a universal law. In fact, the highest vibration, the one vibration always wins, is Love. Love trumps hate. She said so many people have won the battles with the 'Half plus One Rule' outcome that humanity has forgotten there don't need to be battles at all. Because two groups coming together in love, are always stronger. If two groups come together and one loves and one hates, the one with more love wins. So, if this intention would be set forth, then the universal creating spirit would have no choice but to honor the greatest vibrational good.

Again, Satori seemed a little lost. It was a lot to take in and this was day one of what was proving to be a couple of long days. Satori had not had any time to digest anything. She could not believe how much had happened in the last few days. They agreed Satori should go home and take a nap. Darvey was going to come by after work and check on her, anyway. Naoma asked she think about what she told had told her and journal her thoughts and feelings. They would pick back up tomorrow.

Satori still wasn't sure how any of what Naoma just told her was going to help her. Her birthday was tomorrow, and she felt completely unprepared. The only thing she knew for sure was there was a bunch of confusing religious talk Naoma told her to think about and Satori wasn't about to become religious. Still it kind of made sense, and meant it love mattered, so she would think about it.

"Naoma," Satori asked. "What about tomorrow? It's my birthday. You said I am at the greatest risk, or at least that is what you believe. How can what you told me today change the outcome of what tomorrow has in store?"

"Satori, I am going to be honest with you. Nothing I have told you today will change it at all." Naoma replied.

"Then why did you just waste my day. I am in danger and you spend the day talking to me about all these nonsense things that don't even matter and can't help me. We spent the entire day talking about all of this? I need to protect myself for tomorrow."

"These are things you must know if you are to continue learning and growing into a mystic. Which I believe you will. Still, there is only one thing that will stop tomorrow," she said.

"I have to make it through tomorrow, Naoma. That is the first step, not this!" Satori insisted.

"It is your decision if you are going to travel this path or not. You must believe you can win, or you are destined to lose," Naoma retorted.

"Half Plus One, will help determine the victor in the battle you are going to face. I believe if you choose to follow this path, you will be able to impact such a large number of people in the world you will have the plus one on your side," she explained.

"You need to think about if you want to follow the path, not about tomorrow. You need to decide if you are willing to become a Mystic. If you are, you have a chance of winning this battle. If you aren't, if you don't stop thinking only about yourself and tomorrow, you will have no chance." Naoma again tried to make her point.

"Still, there is only now. And in this moment, in that moment you must only know one thing without question, beyond all doubt. You can be victorious. You had a win last night when the men came to get you. You have placed doubt in their minds. That same doubt along with your courage and belief, will determine how tomorrow turns out.

"Both of these things, I cannot teach you. You must go home, sit quietly, and find those answers within yourself. I pray for the sake of Sarah and all the others you can help in this world, your answers are strong, fast, and true," Naoma ended.

Satori was stunned. Speechless. Motionless. Just trying to absorb everything she had just been told.

Naoma reached over and kissed Satori's forehead as she stood to take their tea cups into the kitchen.

She reminded Satori before she left she was not out of danger and should not take off her ring or necklace. She also reminded her she can't share where Sarah is with Darvey or anyone else. Satori wasn't sure how she was going to keep it from Darvey. She just hoped he understood. He did love her after all, right?

Satori went home and called her boss to tell him she was going to be off again tomorrow. Nathan said not to worry it would all still be there when she got back. Then she went and lay down for a nap. Satori didn't remember falling asleep, but she did remember waking up. Darvey had snuggled in behind her and spooned up to her back. He gently kissed her neck and whispered, "Wake up, Kitten."
Satori inhaled him deeply thinking this was the best thing she had smelled in a long time. Since at least that morning. The rustic, woodsy scent was one she knew well.

16 Kiss Me Goodbye

Satori felt complete with Darvey's arm around her as she woke from her nap. The soft cool down comforter engulfed her. It was all around her except for her neck where Darvey had put her head on his arm laid his other arm on her waist. She felt safe; maybe too safe she wondered. She felt as if the entire world could crumble as long as he was holding her and she would be safe. He was this cocoon of comfort and safety where nothing could touch her, no stomach-turning car-driving phantoms, no scary men who couldn't see her, and certainly no Texas sized wrenches. Darvey was her Superman, and she wanted to stay in his arms as long as she could and let the world go on without her until the danger passed. Still, she knew that was a wish of a little girl and not of a woman who needed to put on her superwomen panties and go save the world, well, her world anyway.

Satori was looking forward to tonight; Darvey was

staying over and not on the sofa. What better present could a girl ask for? It was a rare treat to get to wake-up next to Darvey in the morning. Even though he was nearly part of the family, Satori did not want to set a bad example for Sarah. Unless they were engaged, married, or at least decided they were going to be living together, spending the night was off the table when Sarah was home. It was not because she was old fashioned per se, or that they lived in the middle of Bible belt Kansas. It was more because she did not want Sarah to see men rotating in and out of her life and this was one way to make sure it didn't happen.

The couple took a while getting out of bed, being easily distracted with each other's hands and mouths. Teasing, tugging and tickling as if the world wasn't falling apart all around them and Satori didn't have a battle to prepare for. Then Satori heard her stomach growl, and she remembered, it was time to eat.

"I should fix dinner," she whispered as she nibbled his ear, "before your ear is gone completely."

"No need," Darvey responded, "I stopped on the way and got Emperor's."

Excitedly Satori jumped up. "Really?! Did you get me a side of veggies," she questioned hopefully, knowing better than to ask.

"Of course," he said into her neck as he tried to coax her back into bed.

No such luck. As soon as Satori found out her favorite take out was waiting and possibly suffering from loneliness, she was finished with the nibbled hors d'oeuvres in the bedroom. She wanted the main course.

"Desert will wait!" she exclaimed, leaving Darvey puppy eyed. She grabbed his hand and with their hands pretzeled together at the waist they made their way to the kitchen.

They went to the dining room and Satori started setting the table with dishes and serving plates. She decided they were going to pretend she cooked even though they both knew the one meal she couldn't master was fried rice. Every attempt ended in a soggy mush which tasted more like dishwater than rice. She even got out the real chopsticks from her Sushi rolling set. She still hadn't tried to use it and it was going on three Christmas's now.

"So, where is the baby girl?" Darvey asked, "I got her favorite, pot stickers. They are even steamed not fried."

"Oh, she is staying at a friend's house," Satori dismissed. Thinking the brush off was a lot easier than she thought it was going to be.

"You let her out of your sight after yesterday? How do you know she is going to be safe? How was she doing today? She had to be upset after last night." Darvey's questions came at Satori in rapid succession.

Damn it. He isn't going to drop it, she thought to herself.

"She is fine, she has on a little charm to protect her, and she is actually doing rather well. When I left her, she was giggling up a storm." Satori tried to stay dismissive hoping her passivity would help Darvey move on as well.

"So she is staying with her friend Becca then?" he asked.

"No… So, tell me how was your work today? Were things busy for you?" Satori had to try to change the subject herself. She did not know how to tell him she couldn't trust him with this information.

"It was fine, so where is she staying?" he asked again.

"Uhg," she screamed in her head trying not to let it show on her face. He isn't going to drop it. She knew she was just going to have to lean in. Deep breath. Fingers crossed.

"Look Darvey, her safety is the most important thing to me. I cannot tell you where she is staying. Naoma said whoever is after me could use you, without you even knowing it, and find her. I can't take that chance," and then she waited.

"So you think I would hurt her or you or tell someone where she is?" his brow furrowed. "You trust whoever she is with, more than me? You trust Naoma more than me? Have I not proven to you yet how important you and Sarah are to me? Fuck, Satori. What do I have to do?"

Darvey had always been the perfect gentleman, that didn't mean he didn't curse now and then, but Satori couldn't recall him ever using that word before.

"No, I don't think you would. I just cannot take any chances. It's my baby, you know?" Satori's face pleaded with Darvey to let it go, her eyes were angry and hurt. She had never heard him speak like that before, and especially to her.

Darvey stared with intensity for a moment his mouth drawn to a straight line as he gained his composure.

"What about the lessons you had today with Naoma? How did it go?" he asked his plate of food the new question, not wanting to look at Satori this time.

She wished he would just be with her and they could be happy together and not talk and worry about all this stuff. She needed him to be her soft place to land away from the craziness spinning her world out of control. She needed him separate from it all and be available to be her shoulder, and there for her when she needed a kiss. She had to try to convey this without hurting him. She knew men need to be saviors; she had to try to help him understand he could still be her salvation but maybe not in the way he was hoping.

"Look, I just want to be with you tonight and enjoy our time together and forget about everything else going on. Will you please be that for me?" She looked straight at him, lifting his chin to meet her eyes now.

"I was here too." He started. "I was attacked just like Sarah and you. Why don't you care about how this impacts me? Why are making me an outsider? I am on your side, Satori. We are in this together. I need to know what is going on and help fight this with you, not just be your pillow. I feel like I am just a toy you have around to distract you. Honestly, it's pissing me off. Naoma is telling you not to trust me, isn't she?"

"It isn't... Darvey. I just have a lot on my shoulders right now and I really need time to sort it out. You are the perfect distraction; but not if all you want to do is talk about it. If you truly love me - like you say you do - you would understand."

Regret washed over her face as she tried to swallow her words, but they were already out.

"Now you're questioning if I love you?"

Darvey was silent for a moment.

"I only told you yesterday and you are already using it against me... like a weapon... that is not why I told you, Satori. I thought you might love me too," he responded angrily. "I want to be here for you, but not if you aren't going to allow me in. I cannot keep being the odd man out of your girl party." His hand slammed against the table. The emotion in his wide eyes made it clear the fist was more forceful than he had anticipated. "I need some time to think too."

With that, Darvey got up and left, making sure the screen door did not slam with the same force as his fist. He was angry, not mean. He wanted to be able to come back once he cooled off. Or at least have the option.

Satori felt every step across the floor like a dull knife cutting the strings of her heart to his. She was powerless to stop him. She knew this is where everything was headed from the moment the relationship started. He was too good for her, she was not worthy of him. It was only a matter of time before he figured it out.

The wrench, as they say, had hit the fan.

The man who promised to never leave Satori because his mom sent him to her, the man who just twenty-four hours ago confessed his love to her, the man who she too thought she was falling head over heels for, had just left her. Abandoned her. Rejected her. Just like everyone always did, always does. It is always Satori against the world, just like on those stairs when Joyce found her in the basket, abandoned, rejected, and on her own. Again. Now she had to find the strength and courage to fight an impossible battle alone.

That Damned Wrench. Every time.

Just then Satori remembered something Naoma had said, "You receive what you expect to receive."

"No. No. No. I did this." Satori said out loud.

She ran to the door to see if she could catch Darvey, she had to stop him and persuade him to stay, to apologize to him. But she knew the truth before she even got to the door. He was gone. It was too late. She had pushed him away. This perfect wonderful man she had pushed away because that is what she expected to happen. She didn't know if Darvey and their relationship could be saved. But she did know it was going to have to wait until tomorrow.

There was no time to dwell on Darvey. Satori needed to decide what she was going to do. She had two big decisions. First, was she willing to learn the ways of the mystic? Second, did she believe she could win?

She went to bed and began contemplating these questions as she drifted to sleep. Alone in her bed, on the eve of her thirty-eighth birthday. One year after losing her mother and everything else she knew to be true about her life. Feeling assured no matter what tomorrow brought it would be one hell of a birthday.

17 The Darkness

Satori is being chased by a blackness. A chasm. A deep darkness that has no beginning and no end. She can't see where her feet are landing until her foot hits the ground. Then it lights with such brilliance she can't take her eyes off of it. The light throbs and glows all around where she stepped. Each stride lighting with immeasurable beauty. Iridescent glowing waves of ripples expanding without end. She is so mesmerized by the pools she does not even remember she is being chased; she is just running. Running for her life, but also running because it makes her feel alive. She can see a bright light in the distance. It is blinding. It feels like it is rushing toward her unbearably fast yet it never arrives. She reaches for it just as the darkness chasing her catches up.

She turns to look behind her and smoky arms form from every direction, converging into one long strand of a black void. It is not so much black as it is simply gone, more nothing than something. So gone nothing can exist within it. Mesmerized and entranced she can't take her eyes off of the darkness now. She just watches it as it attaches itself to her back. Starting at her shoulders and ending in the curve of her spine, it engulfs her entire frame. She can see the beautiful, brilliant, iridescent aura light that was in front of her, now moving through her like a pinprick of light through the end of a sewing needle. It has entered from the front of her through her heart.

She feels it resisting, but the pull of the darkness is so strong. She is only an observer but still is aware of the feelings of it all. As the light moves through her Satori can feel an immense joy and happiness. From this tiniest of strands moving through the eye of needle sized opening. There is an understanding that the gigantic pools she was landing on while running was amazingly brilliant with even more emotion of the same kind. Like the love and light of 'one hundred forty-four thousand people' were all being shone on her at once. She can look through her own being and see it as it travels from front to back. She is unsure how she can see from her front to her back so clearly and easily and even through herself, as if she has no solid mass, but this doesn't bother her so much as it just pops a question in her mind then out again and she is instantly put at ease.

She realizes she is observing the light pass through her and into the darkness that had attached to her. It was chasing her and then attached to her back, and the light had been in front of her, and now was moving through her. The darkness was absorbing the light into its nothingness. She suddenly understood. The darkness was using her to pull the love and joy she was feeling through her.

This realization woke her from her blissful trans. She started to panic and the light grows brighter more intense and a larger amount is now pulling through. She feels the darkness tighten on her back and it pains her while the light seems to add relief and bliss. Then she hears a call: "WAKE UP!" it seems to shriek and she trembles in her bed.

Her mind begins to wake. She starts to become aware of her physical self. She is lying on her right side, toward the nightstand, but almost on her stomach. Her left knee is hitched up almost to her chin keeping her from being flat on her stomach. Her arms are under her head and pillow. Her back is aching from her neck to her lower spine. She tries to move, but the pain is excruciating. She suddenly realizes she can't move. Something or someone is holding her down. She starts to panic. What is this? she wonders. Why can't I move? She thinks she can move her head just not her body.

She opens her eyes now, trying to determine if she is still in a dream or if she is awake. She can't determine. She thinks she is awake, but she wants to go back to sleep so badly she can barely stay conscious. It is as if she is being pulled to sleep with an equal force of being pulled awake. She drags her eyelids open far enough to allow the glow of the clock on her nightstand to seep in, it says 12:57 a.m. She gets a flash of her birth. She sees the light shining brightly in her eyes from where it had been only darkness before. A man's face. He is almost familiar but she can't really make out his features. Her mind floods and she is back in her room. She knows she must be dreaming.

She works to turn her head, struggling, but her body won't move. It's like her mind is awake but her body is paralyzed. She must see what is holding her in place.

Out of frustration, Satori screams in her mind. Only

rather than in her mind, the sound comes from her mouth. She can tell it came out more like a moan than a scream in her room, but it wouldn't matter, she is alone anyway. Still, she is emboldened by this and tries again to move. She is able to turn her head only. She sees it. The darkness, the same darkness from her dream is there. It is hovering above her like smoke from a pipe or a dry ice machine. Only the smoke is black and the inky blackness is consuming her. She also sees the strand of light just like in her dream coming through her back and into the darkness.

She feels paralyzed. She cannot tell if it is with fear or from what is being done to her. But without a doubt Satori knows she is awake. Still, this can't be real. Is this is what Naoma was telling her about? Is she fighting now? No, she can't be, She is not prepared. She hasn't made her decisions. She doesn't know if she can win. She doesn't think she can. Not yet. Not Now. She feels herself weakening. Like she is being pulled into a deep sleep and she is fighting to keep her eyes open and awake. Her energy is leaving, she can't keep them open anymore. She is falling into a deep sleep and she can't stop it. Her eyes close.

She goes back to the dream. Only this time rather than being chased by the darkness and the light being pulled through her, Satori herself is the light. She feels the brilliance, the love, the hope, the joy. It is overwhelming and so much more powerful and stronger than the darkness was. The darkness is still there only it doesn't have a front or a back, it is all around her, surrounding her. The darkness is absorbing her light from everywhere. The light is being pulled from her like she had been pulled into sleep.

It is as if the needle hole is gone and with it so did any limitations of bliss, Satori can feel so much love it is boundless. However, the darkness can pull the light faster this way as well.

Satori is terrified and ill-prepared. She knows she isn't equipped for this the battle. She has no idea where to start. How do you fight a battle with an enemy you don't know, on a battlefield you have never seen, in a world you know nothing about? There are no weapons, not even words. She is overwhelmed with a feeling of helplessness. She is going to lose. She wishes she could just wake up, but she knows she cannot. More than just this battle, she is going to lose her life, her daughter, everything. This darkness is going to win.

Sarah. She begins to think about Sarah. She thinks about how sad Sarah will be. Who will take care of her? How will this affect the rest of her life? Satori has no idea how Sarah will carry on without her.

Even though she is terrified and scared, she knows she has to figure this out for Sarah. What if the Darkness comes for Sarah next? Satori cannot allow that. Satori wants to fight but doesn't know how and the more she gives in to feelings of helplessness the more light slips from her into the darkness. It is gushing now. Like a dam has broken. All her light is flowing out of her. She gets the sense her light is actually her love. All her love is leaving her. Satori determines if she is going to lose all of her love then she is going to send as much of it to Sarah as she can. She accepts her fate, whatever it may be and pulls up a picture in her mind of her daughter. A beautiful picture of them together last summer when they went to the beach. The sun was shining in the background and they took a selfie with a sandcastle they found, a huge gorgeous sandcastle. It was such a fun day.

She pictured Sarah in her mind and started sending her all the light she had left within her. All the love she could still grasp. She sent it all to Sarah with the intention of filling her to bursting with her love and light. She thought, "I am going to give her every last drop of love I have even if it will be the end of my life."

She didn't care if her light was going to be gone, what mattered is the darkness wasn't going to get it. Her light was going to her daughter. Her love. Her heart. Sarah wasn't going to face this darkness alone like she had to.

Just as the last vestiges of light were draining away she felt the light starting to be pulled back from the darkness. It began traveling back into Satori. She was now pulling it away from the darkness. Satori didn't understand this any more than she understood how or why it was leaving in the first place.

Still, with every bit that came to her she felt more energized, more fight enter her, more desire to win. She wanted to figure out how and why this worked. She wanted to learn the path Naoma was offering her. She wanted to understand Half Plus One. And she wanted to keep feeling the beauty of the aura iridescent brilliant light. She thought for a moment that she could actually win perhaps not all is lost. Just maybe, the darkness does not have control. Naoma told her, love wins, the high vibrating energy is what endures. Half Plus One. When it was just the darkness and her, it was winning because she couldn't imagine how to fight. But when it was The Darkness, Sarah and Satori, her half become a plus one, Sarah. Satori could win. Sarah was her anchor. She realized why it was so important to keep Sarah safe and why they would want to take Sarah from Satori. They knew Sarah could help her win.

Satori determined with her whole being, "I can win. I have no more doubt." Satori felt an awakening within her. Physically, but spiritually as well. She turned her head. The darkness was still above her. However; it was no longer attached to her. She turned over. She looked at it with disdain trying to make some sense of its shape or form when all it really was is smoke. How dare it try to take my light, my life, my love from me? she wondered.

She began seeing a new tendril of inky black smoke come from its body. It was again attaching itself to her right at her temple, but this time she could tell she was doing it. Pulling from it as it had pulled from her. Her anger and resentment had called to it and it recognized the blackness. It came to her in recognition and companionship. It was finding its home in her anger. Satori had taken all of her Light back and now she was taking the blackness into her through her rage.

Horrified at the implications and the thought that she just welcomed this beast, she screamed in agony.

The darkness recoiled and shrieked away. Satori watched as it passed up through the ceiling of her bedroom.

Just then the phone rings, "Mom?!" It was Sarah. Satori's eyes began to water and her voice trembled.

"Yes sweetie, what's wrong?" Satori asks.

"Are you okay, mom? I had a dream you had come to me to say goodbye. You said you needed to give me all of your love before someone took it from you."

"I am fine, Sweetie. It was just a dream," she assured her. There was no reason to get her worked up over the truth. "There is nothing to worry about. Now go back to sleep. We will see each other soon!"

"I love you, Mommy," Sarah responded.

"I love you more my sweet girl." Satori hung up and began to sob.

She was crying uncontrollably as she reached over to where Darvey is supposed to be. Again, she was reminded of her abandonment. Her rejection. The sobs only deepened. She never knew a broken heart could hurt physically until now. No-one was there. Just her. Alone. She also wondered if she was too young to die from a broken heart, she had heard of it happening, but those people were usually older. Nonetheless, the pain in her chest was excruciating. She could barely breathe. Why did she let him leave?

Still, she made it out of the battle even if she is scared and alone. It was so real, she thought. She just can't get over how unlike a dream It was and how actual and real it was. But it couldn't have been, could it? She almost lost her life, and never saw her baby again, she knew this was a truth she couldn't deny. The other truth was what saved her. The love she held for Sarah and Naoma's lessons.

Satori now knew there wasn't a choice. She had to continue learning from Naoma to keep Sarah and herself safe. She didn't know if the darkness was gone. She knew she had won this battle. Satori also knew if it came back she must be better prepared. She knew the darkness now knew her strength and would be ready for her next time. Satori knew it was not giving up, and she knew what it was after. With all of her knowing, she still hoped this would be the last she saw of it.

She was in the middle of her full out pity party, Red puffy face, snot-nosed, horribly ugly cry baby pity party when Satori heard a loud frantic banging on the front door. Banging followed by a frantic Darvey. "Satori! Satori, are you in there?"

She jumped out of bed and went to the door to unlock it before she remembered her face and the fact it looks like someone took a Louisville slugger to her.

Darvey crashed through the front door.

"Are you okay?" he examined her face, her puffing eyes and swollen cheeks. Darvey explained how he was sleeping when something woke him up. He knew Satori was in trouble and agonized he couldn't get to her in time.

He continued to look her over and said he could tell he was too late; Someone had already hurt her.

"Your face! What else did they do? How did you get away?" he asked with concern.

Satori was ejected from her own pity party and back to reality.

"No one beat me up, this is my ugly cry face, you jerk. I am sad because I was alone and this dark 'thing' came," motioning circles with her hands all around herself and toward her back. "And I and had to fight it alone, and you left me alone. Did I mention I was alone?" Satori looked up at him with a furrowed brow, pouty lips, and the best angry face she could muster, as happy as she was to see him.

It was near impossible for Darvey not to laugh at the combination of puffy ugly cry face and angry face together. Satori looked a lot like one of the puffer fish in the Chinese buffet fish tanks. His strong arms gathered her in tight rubbing her back and squeezing her, hoping she didn't see the smile on his face.

Darvey held her close to him as they sat on the sofa. Satori was still trembling and crying. Still overwhelmed. He asked her how she was able to get away from it, the darkness, as she was calling it. Satori explained how she started sending all the love she had left to Sarah because she worried about how she would survive without her mom. The thought terrified her. This somehow made the darkness go away. She didn't understand why. Darvey kissed her forehead.

"I am so sorry I left, Satori," He confessed. "I was hurt, I felt like you were leaving me out and I want to be part of your life. I want to be involved in every moment of your life. I understand you were worried about Sarah. My leaving almost cost you your life. I will never forgive myself. Can you ever forgive me?"

Satori looked up into his dark brown eyes and kissed him. There were no words. Of course, she forgave him. Satori needed Darvey in her life as much as he needed her. They fit perfectly together. His arm, her neck, his chest, her torso; they knit so easily together as if the heavens had molded them from the same piece of clay. And the spark when they kissed, from the first time they touched it had always been there. Their lips rounded each other's with symmetry and chemistry.

Darvey picked Satori up in her favorite green and teal maxi night dress and carried her back to bed.

They woke the next morning their bodies facing each other with their arms and legs intertwined. Naked bodies touching every possible way without being on top of each other. When Satori opened her eyes, Darvey was staring right into her blue-green-yellow eyes. He had his half-cocked smile on his face.

"You are so beautiful when you sleep. Thank you for letting me be part of your life, Kitten."

Satori smiled back, "How could it be any different, I love you."

With that, they started kissing again. It wasn't long before Darvey's hands found the parts of her body that longed for his touch. They were one again, always. It was magical. They were magic together.

18 An Education

Satori was lying with her head on his shoulder and her leg across his legs, her arm over his chest. Her fingers were tracing the lines of his chest and gently caressing his face, following his brow, the arch of his nose, along his chin. She loved outlining his face as if she were trying to memorize every feature in case he ever went away. She would rub his temples and massage his neck, trying to release his stress and pressure.

"I suppose we should get up. You have to get work and so do I," Satori murmured. "And I need to stop by Naoma's. No telling what she has been going through since last night. I'm sure she felt it too if both you and Sarah did."

Darvey agreed. They went in to shower and then got dressed for the day. Darvey left around seven since he had to go home and change before going into the office. Satori went next door to check in with Naoma.

She was already at the door with a cup of coffee waiting.

"Get in here! I have been so worried about you," she exclaimed.

Satori was not prepared for what she walked into. Naoma had set up her coffee table with a huge display of - well - stuff. There were crystals and herbs and branches, and all kinds of scents in the air.

"What is all this?" Satori was amazed as she looked around and noticed more and larger items like crystals in the corners of the room; realizing it was not restricted to the coffee table.

"This was the battlefield my dear. I knew I could not tell you it was coming or you would have been too unsure or perhaps afraid of what you had to do. You were anyway, and we almost lost you," Naoma responded.

"We need to get started on your education. As I am sure you have guessed this battle is not over. It has barely begun. It is finished for now, but once he can regroup and try again, he will be back"

"Who will?" Satori asked thinking Naoma must have figured out who is after her and her Sarah.

"The darkness, it came for you last night. It will be back. You didn't think you had won did you?" Naoma surprised Satori knowing already how she guessed deep inside it wasn't over.

"Well, I hoped. I mean it shrieked away." Satori faltered.

"Now he knows who he is fighting and you need to be better prepared. He will be as well."

"How do you know it is a he?" said Satori.

"From the energy, It is strong with male undertones. Whoever is after you knows more than he should about how powerful you can be. We need to get started. You are already far behind."

"Tonight I suppose. Sarah is still going to be with Nicole until Saturday. That gives us a little time to work without interruption," Satori said.

"Good," Naoma agreed. "I need you to do

something for me today. I am going to give you some books. Read them when you have a chance. As I said, we have a lot of work to get done. I think we have a few months at least before he tries again. It will either be three or six months, I would guess."

"How do you know?" Satori asked.

"It has to do with the equinox, there is more power then, he doesn't possess his own obviously, or he would be able to come anytime, that or he is using your strength. My fear is, if he chooses six months, then Sarah could also be in danger."

"It will be her birthday!" Satori exclaimed.

"Exactly."

"So, if you can sense it is a male energy, do you think you can find him? Such as, who he is and where he is. Maybe we can bring the fight to him rather than waiting on him to come to us." It sounded reasonable to Satori. She was finished playing the victim all time, just sitting around waiting for wrenches to launch themselves at her. She never again wanted to feel as she did as she woke up last night.

"Yes, I think it's a very good idea. I am going to work on that as well as trying to find your parents. I think it is fair to say we know who was following you now. We just need to figure out why and who they are," Naoma agreed. "We are going to get through this Satori. You cannot have any doubt. Promise me! Do you trust me?"

"Yes of course I do. More than anyone," Satori responded, although she was wondering why Naoma kept asking this same question.

"Good. Nevertheless, remember; don't place all your trust in me or anyone else. The only truth is in your own heart," Naoma reminded her.

"So you're saying I can't trust you?" Satori didn't need this complication right now, she needed a rock, a solid foundation. She needed somewhere she could put all of her faith and trust.

"You can. I am just saying you should not trust me more than you trust yourself. More than you trust what God, Spirit, Universe, whatever you are comfortable saying, tells you; makes you feel is true. Always trust your own instincts and heart above anything you are told.

"As you travel this path, you need to take notes and write about your feelings and experiences. Also, I need you to remember something Satori," Naoma handed Satori a black leather bound journal with an inscription on the front:

You are stronger than you think,
braver than you imagine, and
more capable than you believe.
YOU are descended from greatness and
have the power to create and
manifest everything you desire.
No matter how big or small.
No matter how positive or negative.
No matter how true or false.
Believe in love,
in truth,
in the goodness within you.
You are worthy of all beautiful things.

"Oh, it's beautiful. Thank you, Naoma!"

"When is the last time you read the bible?" Naoma asked.

"I don't know, probably elementary school," Satori

guessed.

"Well, start your reading there. Remember there are tools which point to the truth but ultimately they are only tools. There is no way for someone else to describe the truth to you. Read it with new eyes. With an open mind and an open heart."

Naoma also gave Satori some other books: A New Earth from Eckhart Tolle. Energy Anatomy by Caroline Myss. The Alchemist by Paulo Coelho. And another pile of books entitled The Law of One by Ra.

"So what exactly am I supposed to be learning from all these books?" Satori asked.

Naoma explained the first step is understanding the basic laws or rules. How you need to understand and believe it is possible to manifest anything you want or need. Belief is the most important component. In fact, without belief, true soul-deep understanding, you cannot accomplish anything. We create our life. Everything we think or believe manifests into reality. We must work through the process and have patience. There is much more to learn, however, these books will serve as a beginning to the possibilities to what can be. Still, you must always follow your own heart and path.

It was confusing and overwhelming. Satori believed what happened so far, and she trusted Naoma. She was on-board. Satori took her new book collection and returned home. She left the books on the entryway divider and went to get her bible. It is what she was most comfortable with.

"I am starting with God," she thought.

She started her car and drove to work knowing the journey ahead was much more than reading a couple books. It was heavy and scary. It was long and dark.

But just like the pinpoint of light which seeped through, she knew she had the power to overcome what was headed her way. She knew she had the love of her daughter, she had the love of a beautiful and caring man, and she had the love of a woman who cared for her and her daughter like a mother even though she had lost her mother. These recent months had been as dark as they had been light. Just like the battle she faced last night, and in the end, love won.

Satori drove knowing and believing she could still win, she could still overcome. She knew she had to. She somehow knew this was even bigger than just her and Sarah, this was something more. She did not know what, she didn't know why, she didn't know how. She just knew she had all the right people in her corner and she was going to make it through this education, find this darkness, and win this battle.

So, when her stomach lurched and her eyes automatically flew to her rear view mirror, it wasn't fear that filled her eyes as they glimpsed the Impala. It was determination and courage. Only her courage must have removed a mask because she could now see the face. The face of the man in the car.

She still didn't know who he was, but she did know one thing. When she was in the battle and her eyes drew open, she flashed back to the moment of her birth. There was a fissure of light, the face she saw that was familiar in a way she couldn't understand. She saw this man's face. He was younger, but it was him she had no doubt.

In Satori's mind, there were only two possibilities; the car following her was the person who helped her mother give birth or her father. Either way, this was also the person who now wanted her power. No matter the cost.

www.ingramcontent.com/pod-product-compliance
Lightning Source LLC
Chambersburg PA
CBHW032001170626
46807CB00006B/2590